MISCEGENIST SABISHII
BW/AM IR Romance

PEPPER PACE

Miscegenist Sabishii

BW/AM IR Romance

Pepper Pace

Miscegenist Sabishii

Miscegenist Sabishii

ISBN-13: 978-1480205239

Reviews for Miscegenist Sabishii

"Another sizzling love story by Pepper Pace and as expected she leaves you pining for the next book."
-Karen Green-Berry, Building Relationship Around Books Online Club

"This was a wonderful book one that shows me that love has no color, love is just love."
-Dharp, APB Perspective Reviews

SABISHII (Japanese): Lonely; lonesome; desolate; solitary

MISCEGENATION: The mixing or blending of race in marriage or breeding, interracial marriage. The analysis of emotions, reactions, and anxieties held by people about interracial couplings

FOREWARD

This story originally appeared on Literotica.com as three short stories, which showed the evolution of this couple. Due to the many comments and requests the story was extended after book 1.

Three books later the entire trilogy has been transformed into one novel length story. I would like to thank all of my fans and followers for their many comments and feedback.

Table of Contents

Part I

What we think we become.
-Buddha

TONY

I guess you could say my mom is prejudiced, although she just sees it as preserving her culture. But I'm Japanese American. That is both Japanese and American.

Bringing home non-Asian friends would cause her to refer to them as Big-American-Oxen. So during High School I didn't even think about having a girlfriend. The reason is like that song says; "I like big butts and I cannot lie." Translation; I like black females. But me bringing home a black girlfriend was just never going to happen.

I grew up in a predominately black neighborhood and went to an all black school and as a result I was attracted to the girls that I saw everyday, black girls. My preference was dark skinned, big bootie girls, the more bodacious the better. Does that sound prejudiced? As if it is a fetish? It just means that you don't yet understand that just because I am Asian on the outside doesn't mean that culturally I am not every bit African American.

Oh, and by the way, if we are speaking of stereotypes let me clarify; I am Japanese not Korean. Not all Asians that live or work in all black neighborhoods are Korean. And NO, my parents do not own a hair care store or run a Chinese restaurant! When I speak about my own miscegenistic desires it is

1

not in an attempt to be racist. I like dark skin. I like big butts. Unfortunately, growing up in an urban black neighborhood and going to an all back school meant people saw me as the stereotypical Asian with an identity crisis. But, what do you do, when you feel black and look Asian?

Growing up I talked like my friends, listened to hiphop and rap music, and liked the same sistas that my boys in high school did. But I never got any play. The sistas were not trying to bring a little Asian boy home to meet moms and pops. Even when I wrestled and bulked up the girls would give me the up and down, but every time I'd try to rap to them it would always end up the same way; I'd hit a brick wall and fall flat on my face. And for the record, you have no concept of being dissed until you are dissed by a sixteen-year old black girl.

I did date some in High School. I dated this little blonde white girl for a while, but she dumped me for a black kid that still sucked his thumb in the 10th grade.

In college I finally got mine. Jackie Chan and Jet Li movies were real popular and so was I. I made up for lost time in college, but two years later ... guess what? It got old for me. Yes, sex with random beautiful girls gets old when you want it to go somewhere but you discover that they don't. I am now the fetish and the experiment and the secret.

I discovered that I desired romance much more then sex with big bootie black girls. So while I was hoping for a long-term relationship, my girlfriends were still not trying to take a rap music-listening-to Asian home to meet the parents. For them it was just the curiosity of sleeping with someone outside of their race. I did not see black women as being outside of my race. In my mind I'm every bit as black as my friends.

Now I'm a thirty-three year old mortgage broker that lives alone — except for my dog, Wu-Tang.

I work in a semi-conservative office, so when SHE walked in through the door she had every bit of my attention. Unfortunately trying to step to her wouldn't be easy. But on the plus side none of the other males that work with me would be stepping to her, either. The obstacle for me being that she would be working under me. But for them--well, they are all blue-eyed, Armani suit-wearing types and she walked in looking like Queen Latifah.

Discreetly I checked her out despite the fact that she was twice my size. But from that weaved ponytail that sat at the top of her head to the silver painted nail polish that her open-toed shoes revealed I was hooked.

Julia from personnel introduced us. "Toi," don't laugh, that is my name, "I want to introduce you to the new assistant broker. Toi Yakamoto, this is Nikita Mason."

I shook her hand. Her nails were manicured and the same shade of silver as her toes. She was wearing a grey skirt that hugged her fuller figure cut right above the knee, a pearl pink blouse that accentuated her ample cleavage, and a grey matching suit jacket. I appraised everything from corporate sexy clothing to the silver polish that spoke of a need to be daring. Also, her make-up was flawless. Yes, I appreciate a woman that pampers herself and I could tell that Miss Mason did, and not just because she had shown up on her first day at the office looking on point.

"Miss Mason." I asked innocently. "Is it Miss?"

"Yes. Nikki is fine."

I cut my eyes at Julia before returning my attention to Nikki. "Not many people call me Toi or Mr Yakamoto. Just call me Tony."

Back in my younger days everyone called me T-Baby. Back then everybody had a nickname. Julian was Jay-Dog. Dean was Big Daddy-D. There was Budda, and well ... we were young. People at my office wouldn't know anything about having a nickname like T-Baby, but Nikki might.

Julia left me in charge of showing Nikki the ropes since I would be her team leader. We don't like using the word 'supervisor' here. We are all a team, haha. Anyways, there was pretty much a lull in the day so I decided to drag it out. First stop, the canteen.

"So this is where we keep the vending machines, refrigerator and microwave if you like to bring your lunch. But there are plenty of fast food restaurants in the general vicinity." I led her out of the small room. "Have you done this type of work before?"

"A little" she said in a naturally husky voice, "I've been a real estate agent for three years."

"A real estate license will take you far in this business." I lead her to an empty office. "I guess this is where you'll be hanging your shingle." Nikki's mouth opened in surprise.

"I get my own office?"

"It looks more professional to the clients than sending them to a cubicle."

"Wow," she said, looking around. Since she was in a good mood I decided to make my move.

"Lunch is in about ten minutes. If you'd like to join me over a burger, I'll fill you in on the ropes." Her eyes met mine and I gave her an innocent smile.

"Thanks. That would be great. I've been filling out paperwork all morning and haven't had time for even a cup of coffee."

I took Nikki to a popular cafe within walking distance of the office. She was wearing heels but knew how to work them. During the walk I told her about the company hoping that we could focus on more personal conversation during the meal. Unfortunately she enthusiastically asked question after question about her new position, which kept everything professional.

"... you know those companies that hold the closing fees are skyrocketing. How do you guys feel about completely absorbing those fees, even from the back end?"

I raised my brow. "It would cut out some commission but it could make us more competitive."

Nikki dabbed her lips with her napkin. "People are savvier, Tony. They know about all the tricks we use to inflate the fees." I liked the way she said my name so easily. I even liked the point she was making.

But the executive board wasn't going to be that forward thinking. The Board was creative in finding more ways to hide fees—not trying to be up front about them.

"Nikki, this company has found a comfy little niche with customers well-off enough to disregard our extra fees but not so rich as to hire a slew of tax attorneys to loophole their way through them." Nikki smiled at me like there were a million things she wanted to throw at me, but professional courtesy stopped her from it.

"We're bottom feeders, okay?" I continued, not sure why I admitted that to her. "But I don't have to look into the eyes of some poor old lady dipping into here widow's pension. Our customers are the Baby Mama's of some professional ball player or the bank president's ex-wife."

"Not the bank president or the pro ball player?" She interjected.

"Generally, no." Good God, I hoped that she was not the Baby's Mama to some ball player. And why in the hell had I admitted all of that to her? Maybe because once upon a time I had been something other than that evil corporate figure head that the rest of the world warns against.

On the short walk back to the office, I was finally able to get my wish and find out some personal info about her. "Is Cincinnati your home town?" I asked.

"Born and raised. I grew up in Lincoln Heights, graduated from Walnut Hills."

"Me; Bond Hill, I graduated from the School of Creative and Performing Arts-"

"Bond Hill!" She asked, head swivelling, unable to hide her shock. Bond Hill is considered a "nice hood", nice houses, tree-lined streets—but still the hood and virtually all black.

"You don't know Julian Beatty, do you?"

"Jay-Dog? Yeah we used to get-" I almost said high. " … into a lot of mischief Friday nights." Julian was one of my very best friends but we'd lost touch after I'd gone off to college.

"That's my cousin!" She yelled happily and a few passer-bys turned to look at her curiously, but she didn't even notice.

"No!" I laughed. "What's my boy been up to?" I started sliding easily into the familiar vernacular.

"Married, two kids and still D.J'ing on the weekends."

"God, are you serious?"

"He's still the best D.J. in the city ... well in my humble opinion. You know he has a regular gig playing clubs."

"No, I didn't know that. Where?"

"Club Ritz on Old School Sundays."

I laughed in genuine pleasure. "I gotta check him out." Club Ritz used to be my spot!

Nikki gave me a long look. "I can't believe you grew up in Bond Hill." She seemed to see me for the first time. "What was it like growing up in the hood with a name like Toi?"

I smirked. "I wouldn't know. No one from the neighborhood knows my real name." I remembered agonizing at the beginning of each school year when the teacher called out roll, hoping that the forged note I'd sent to school would take care of making sure my name was listed as Tony. "Honestly, when I did take my friends home they thought my mom was calling me Tony — you know, with the accent and all."

Nikki burst out laughing and we walked into the building having to stifle the sound. "I like you Tony." She said while going into her office.

I straightened my tie.

Half-way there.

Nikki

I've made one friend at work, Tony Yakamoto. Other than that, the people are the same cold corporate types that worked at the real estate agency I quit. I made good money there but I needed more. More job fulfilment I guess, I don't know. So I started looking for something different and the salary was right. So here I am.

Although I've never done refinancing this work is familiar. Anybody can do it—but it takes a person with a real estate license to legally sign or quote numbers. Tony has made the training very easy but this place is a world away from my prior job downtown in the city. Then, my customers were mostly black, as were my co-workers.

The ladies I now work with invite me to eat lunch with them but I would much rather NOT. It's not that I don't like them, but all they talk about is shit I'm not even trying to be interested in; like sorority sisters, forty dollar t-shirts at the GAP, vacations in the mountains and boyfriends named Todd and Beau. Hell, I'm not struggling financially, but there is no way that I would shell out forty dollars for a t-shirt! You see in my circle we brag about how much cute shit you can buy for a hundred bucks.

And the last vacation I took was a shopping spree at the outlet shops in Tennessee. Believe me when I say that my friends and I didn't stay in a chalet, but a seventy-dollar a night motel off the strip where my friends and I pushed the beds together and slept in a pile. As for Todd and Beau ... let's just say that all men seem to be thinking about these days is hittin' it and quittin' it.

Most times I end up having lunch with Tony. At first I thought it might come off as peculiar to others but no. Tony is just that down to earth that he is easy to hang out with. He's a young Asian dude who I first thought was trying to act too familiar with my race. You know how people do; I'm referring to white people.

They think they are showing how comfortable they are with your culture by testing out their slang-knowledge. But it just comes off making them look stupid and leaving you feeling awkward. 'I told him I'm just not down with that.' 'Oh my God I saw this purse that was so phat! It was sick!'

Please white people ... don't do that.

But Tony is not like that. He actually is black! I know it's strange because he is a short Asian but he grew up in Bond Hill and happens to be best friends with my all time favorite cousin, Julian—who I call Jay.

In some ways work is like being in school and trying to make new friends. Tony is probably the only one I could really consider a friend. And that's because he never switches hats on me. He can give me direction as my supervisor then ask me if I want to take a break with him and one of the Board of Directors. That's what's so cool about him. He can hang out comfortably at the top and schmooze with the tax attorneys just as easily as he can sit across from me at a burger joint.

And listen to this—his nickname was T-Baby. This I learned from Jay. You can't get blacker than a nickname like that. Jay told me to watch out because Tony liked black women with big asses and big titties which I happen to have an ample amount of both. I told Jay he should be happy that we were talking over the phone and I couldn't pop him in the head. Tony is at least a foot shorter than me and I have about 50 pounds on him, so there was nothing happening there even if he wasn't my team leader.

I can say that I've warmed up to the job a lot. I especially love Fridays—not only because it's the end of the workweek, but because it is dress down day and I can be more myself. This Friday I decided to wear a sheer cream blouse, billowy and ethereal, over a spaghetti string tea length dress that hugged me in just the right spots. The cover-all made me appear demure and though beneath it I was rocking a skintight skirt I thoroughly pulled off the 'corporate sexy' look. I realize that I'm a bit flamboyant. But I am still tasteful.

First thing Fridays we have meetings for like two hours. People bring things to snack on. Tony doesn't drink coffee so he always brings a good Asian tea and almond cookies. I don't even eat the donuts and danishes anymore, the cookies and tea are that good.

After two months I just finally had to know and so I asked. "Where do you get these?" I was on my third cookie.

"I make them."

"Are you serious?" He shrugged. "They're not hard to make."

"I bet your girlfriend loves and hates you for this," I said while munching a heavenly cookie. He gave me a quick look then laid out more cookies on a tray.

"It's just me and Wu-Tang."

"Wu-Tang?"

"My dog; my boxer."

I chuckled. "Wu-Tang. That's a cool name."

"Did you get some of the tea?"

"Did you make that too?" I said, half joking.

"Yes, I actually did. I blend the leaves myself."

"Jeez Tony … " I gave him an impressed stare. Then Mr Milton called the meeting to order.

Later that day Tony asked me to go to The Ritz with him to watch my cousin D.J. on Old School Sunday. At first I didn't know how to take the invite, but Tony was just cool like that and I'm sure he wouldn't make it into something that it wasn't. Besides, he's a little man and I'm tall and thick—not necessarily fat, but what a man would call healthy. So I told him that it would be cool and I'd call Jay to let him know we were coming. Tony told me he'd pick me up, which at first I objected to but he assured me that it would be right en route to the club, so I okayed it.

TONY

So after two months of working together Nikki and I have a date. Okay, actually, it wasn't a date but I was going to use tonight as an opportunity to tell her that I liked her—out of the work place where it wouldn't seem like sexual harassment.

I drive a Jag. My big weakness is that I like nice things. I own a nice condo, drive a nice car, and wear expensive clothes. Nikki has never seen me dressed casually, not even on dress down Fridays.

Tonight I did, donning black slacks and a black shirt that stretched across my torso and arms allowing all of the work that I've been doing in the gym to show. I was also sporting black Timberlands and a Kokopelli necklace.

I got to Nikki's place early so that she could let me in while she finished getting ready and then I could scope out her living arrangements—but she had me beat because she wasn't on CP time.

I didn't even care because she looked so damn good. What Nikki's wardrobe had hinted at work was now all up in my face. Baby had cleavage for miles! She was wearing a spaghetti string dress that went just below her knees, ankle strap heels and a hair weave that fell exotically down her back. Forget trying to play it cool because my mouth hung open and my tongue rolled out and practically hit the floor!

"Did I over dress?"

"N-no." I stuttered. "You look great." I led her out to the car, opening the passenger door for her.

"Tony!" She exclaimed. "Your ride is sharp!"

"Thanks." I started the car and the radio came on already tuned to the local R&B station. Out of the corner of my eye I watched her make a silent assessment of my environment--and me.

I think I'm three quarters of the way there.

The club wasn't crowded. There was a nice older group, mostly black but still a good mixture of races. The conversation on the ride over was mostly about what clubs and bars we liked. Nikki had never been to the Ritz before so I led us in and directly to VIP. I hadn't been there in years but the bartended recognized me and we slapped hands and talked for a few moments before continuing upstairs to VIP.

When we got there I was surprised to see a group of friends that I hadn't seen since my college days. "Hell no! Big D?!" I yelled hugging Dean. He was the one 'Big American Ox' that used to come to my house on a regular basis.

"T-Baby!" He said equally as enthusiastically, slapping my back heavy-handedly. My entire crew was here. Back in high school we used to be practically inseparable. I greeted each of them enthusiastically and then everyone stood back, looking at Nikki and me together curiously. I'm sure they were wondering if we were 'together'. I pulled her forward

"Hey guys, this is Nikki, Jay-Dog's cousin." And then they greeted her enthusiastically, too. Dean gave me an inquisitive look that I ignored because I really didn't know how to respond. Nikki wasn't really with me but ...

"Where is Jay-Dog?" I asked while pulling out a chair for Nikki then sitting down next to her.

"He's in the middle of a set." I let my head bob to the rhythm of his slamming beat. "He's still good." I looked at Nikki. "Did you know about these guys being here?"

She beamed at me. "Jay told me not to say that he was inviting the entire gang."

"None of us knew." Dean said and then gave Nikki an appreciative once over. Thankfully she didn't notice. We ordered drinks, Nikki ordered Hennessey — I stuck with soda since I had made myself her designated driver. Nikki got comfortable with everybody. Whether it was the Hennessey or because she had a connection with them through her cousin, I don't know, but it was nice being with her and knowing that she was at ease with my friends.

I was relieved when Jay-Dog came back from the D.J's booth. And not just because I hadn't seen him in forever, but because Dean caught Nikki's attention and he was trying to engage her in some one on one dialogue.

To Dean's credit he is what most women would be attracted to; 6'3", shaved head, goatee, and a body that showed his love of weight lifting. But even back in our high school days I knew that he was an even bigger dog than Wu-Tang.

When Jay-Dog left the D.J. booth and entered VIP he started ragging on me because I had bulked up a lot since he'd last seen me. I told him that he had gained the fat that I had lost, and then I rubbed his Buddha belly. It was all in fun. I was heavier from my years in the gym and even though my people are not blessed in the gluteus maximus area; the stair master took over where nature fell short. I'm also proud to say that my shirt outlined my triceps and biceps quite nicely.

"Nikki, you should have seen T-baby in high school." Jay-Dog was saying. "He was skinny, and was always sportin' these mirrored sunglasses."

The guys roared.

"I still got those things. They're going to come back in style," I joked.

"This is the only Japanese dude in the world who ever wore his pants hanging off his ass."

"You didn't do that?!" Nikki asked, amazed.

"Only long enough for my mom to yank them down and beat my ass in public. After that I lost my taste for it."

Jay-Dog had to go back into the booth and before Dean could swoop in on Nikki again, I asked her if she wanted to dance. She gave me a surprised look then led me to the dance floor. Some booty-bouncing song was on and all of the women on the dance floor were making me feel like I was in a rap video.

But instead of bouncing her ass, Nikki raised her hands over her head, closed her eyes and let her body sway to the beat of the song. She wasn't dancing like anyone else and looked damn good doing what she was doing. I stepped up closer to her but not enough to actually touch and then I matched her moves like a silhouette. She brought one arm down to my shoulder and I put my hand on her hip. I closed my eyes, too, matching her moves by the feel of her swaying hips.

When the song changed I opened my eyes to see her watching me. Her eyes were glossy from the Hennessy, but she looked like she was enjoying herself on the dance floor. She suddenly changed her dancing, clapping her hands and gyrating her voluptuous body. Her breasts were catching a lot of attention from other guys on the dance floor — not just me.

I broke out in my own moves and Nikki gave me an impressed look. Back in the day I used to live in clubs, if I know nothing else I know how to dance. When Nikki saw that I was at ease on the dance floor, something seemed to transform in her. She dropped it like it was hot and began to lay claim to the dance floor.

She and I danced song after song until J-Dog slowed it up. Nikki turned to head back to VIP but I took her hand and pulled her to me. She smiled and put her arms around my neck so that I could hold her hips. With her wearing high heels my eyes were even with her mouth and I didn't want to have to look up at, her making me feel even shorter than I already was. But I couldn't look down either, because ... well, her breasts were there.

So I turned my head to the side and before I knew what I was doing I had my face in the crook of her neck. Instead of pushing me away, she lessened the slack of her arms around my neck, causing our bodies to come together closer and now we were actually dancing close enough to be one! I was pleased. We were slow dancing.

When the song ended she quickly slipped away from me and headed for the ladies room. I went back to the table and ordered her a fresh drink.

Dean winked at me. "That your lady, man?"

I paused. "Not yet." Dean laughed. "That's a fine sista. You think you can handle that?"

I gave him a knowing grin. High school was over, and I might not have as many notches on my belt as he had ... but I could hold mine. When Nikki came back I tried to scope out how she was feeling about the dance, but her expression showed nothing. I was happy to see my boys and all, but because they were there it took away the intimate quality that I had been hoping for. Still, I was having a good time and she seemed to as well. "Nikki, let me know when you're ready to go."

She looked at her watch. "In and hour?"

"Okay."

My boys tried to get her to dance with them because she was the only female in the group, but she begged off, complaining that her feet were bothering her. I wanted to offer to give her a foot massage since I was a licensed masseuse, but since I had never even told her that I liked her, I didn't think it would be very cool to be rubbing on her feet. Yes, in my prior life I used to enjoy a living as a massage therapist.

I went to the restroom and when I came back Dean and Nikki had their heads together chuckling. They straightened when they saw me. Damn, Dean was blocking my flow ...

"You ready to go?" I asked even though the hour wasn't up.

"Yeah." She stood up and we all said our goodbyes, promising to hook-up next month at the basketball court. When we exchanges phone numbers I kept my eye on Dean making sure he didn't secretly slip his to Nikki. I decided I was going to fuck him up on the court when I saw him again. Not only can I dance, I can play some mean basketball.

Back in the jag Nikki sighed tiredly. "You have some nice friends." She yawned.

"Did you have fun?"

"I did. You did too."

"Yeah that was a nice surprise. You hungry? I know I am."

"I can't eat this late at night."

"Are you for real? How can you go out drinking and not hit White Castles after?"

"Uh ... That would be the desire not to puke two hours later. Besides, there's work tomorrow and it's already after midnight."

"Yeah you're right," I responded disappointed. This wasn't going the way I had planned it; Woo Nikki with my wit and personality. Tell her I liked her and then challenge her arguments against inter-office romances.

At her house she patted my arm good night and let herself out the door before I could make a move to open it for her. Not even a good night peck on the cheek. I'm not a pessimist—but I know when the odds are   stacked   against   me.

NIKKI

Man, my head was pounding. Why in the hell did I order Hennessy — straight up? I guess I felt a little nervous. But then every time someone bought a round of drinks they'd order me another one. I ain't gonna lie; I was fucked up for a hot minute. I remember Tony asking me to dance and he was so good out on the dance floor that I reverted back to my Hoochie mama days. That was the most fun I've had in a long time. Tony grabbed me for a slow dance and you know ... it felt so good being held. Afterwards I went to the bathroom and cried. Isn't that crazy?

There was this brother Dean there. He is F-I-N-E! Brother couldn't keep his eyes off me. I wanted to get to know him but somehow it didn't seem right to rap to another man when you come with someone else — even if that someone else was just Tony and he wouldn't have cared. But still ...

The next day at work Tony brought me Perrier after taking one look at my red-rimmed eyes. And somehow I made it through the day. At home I planned to strip down naked and climb into bed but there was a message on my answering machine. Imagine my surprise when I heard Dean's voice! He hoped I didn't mind that he had gotten my number from my cousin Jay and blah ... blah ... blah! I whooped loudly when he said he'd like to take me out sometime and he left his phone number.

The next day Dean and I talked on the phone for hours. We had so much in common! We made a date for that Friday and we talked every night on the phone. He kept asking me about Tony, though.

"Ain't nothing going on between you and ol' T-baby is it?"

"What? No," I said surprised. "He's my supervisor at work. Team leader is what they like to call it, whatever."

"Oh. Well why are you going out with your supervisor?" I frowned at the phone.

"Because he's friends with Jay. We weren't going out, we were just hanging out" There is a difference. "Why? Is there something wrong with Tony?"

"Naw. It's just when I saw T roll up with you on his arm it surprised me. Tony never got no play in High School. Dude always went for the black chicks, but they were too busy trying to get with me." He laughed. I thought that was mean so I changed the subject.

Friday we went to see a movie and to dinner. Dean is sexy and I'm not going to lie, I was horny and I gave him some. It's been so long since I've been touched that I was exploding in 5 minutes! It was good and everything, don't get me wrong, but Dean spent a lot of time trying to make himself look sexy. You can tell when a man is trying to star in his own porno.

Come Monday I planned to ask Tony about Dean but he beat me to it. He asked me what I did over the weekend.

"I went out with your boy Dean. We saw a movie and then went out to dinner."

"Dean ... " He said surprised. Tony's lip curled up, but he wasn't smiling. "So did you have a good time?"

"Yeah. He's cool."

"That's good." He walked out of the office singing softly to himself. I think it was that Amy Winehouse song where she asks what kind of fuckery is this.

TONY

I've been spending so much time at the gym that regulars think I work there. Someone has already asked me if I would take them on as a personal trainer. I always liked the gym, but since Nikki started seeing Dean I have a lot of pent up aggression that I'm trying to get rid of. I spend like four hours a night there!

My mom is still trying to hook me up with Asian women. She's gone through the daughters, granddaughters, nieces, and cousins of all of her Asian friends. So she's taken to picking women up off the street for me.

I went over for Sunday dinner and she had a lady there that she'd met at the nail salon. She was Korean, not even Japanese! I did take her out but she kept commenting that I sounded like I was black. I finally told her my real dad was mulatto and she excused herself to go to the bathroom and never came back.

My cousin Noonie has wanted to detail my car since I got it. She works for an auto dealership where she does detailing on the weekends. Nice things always made me feel better so I let her take it one day, which started turning into a monthly thing. I suspect that she's using the opportunity to drive around the city in it. But I don't actually care because Noonie does great work and she's not charging me a dime so she can knock herself out. On the days she takes the car she drops me off at work, picks me up and then I take her out to eat. After I drop her off at her place I hit the gym. This is now my life. Crap.

Nikki and me were walking out of the office together one day and she stopped when she saw my car parked at the curb.

"Isn't that your car?"

"Yup." Noonie had just tinted the windows. She climbed out of the driver's seat sporting spiked fuchsia hair, a short schoolgirl skirt, fishnets and combat boots. My Aunt no longer even tries to find her a nice Asian Boy.

She tossed me the keys. "How do you like?" She asked then danced around the sidewalk. There wasn't even the smallest bubble.

"Nice. I like. For this you get steak tonight." I waved goodbye to Nikki and Noonie and I drove off to Ruth's Chris steakhouse.

NIKKI

Dean was telling me how I should get rid of my retirement plan because it was stupid to save for a future that wasn't even promised to us and people were stupid to go without when they had thousands collecting dust in the bank.

I was in a sour mood today so I didn't even bother to argue with him. Why do men always have to act like they know more than they do? Goddamn! I have a college degree, my own home, a car and I don't need some man's advice. Especially not from someone who plays video games all day. Don't get me wrong, I like Dean … but in short spurts.

My thoughts reverted back to the girl that was driving Tony's car. It looks like he's been getting some. He never even mentioned her and I thought we were buddies. This skinny Asian woman's been driving his car and picking him up from work. Then on Friday he didn't even bring the cookies or tea. When I asked him what was up with that he shook his head in a distracted way.

That night Dean didn't show up for our date. I waited for two hours for him to pick me up before calling his cell phone—which he never answered. Shit, I was tired of him anyway. The next day he showed up at my door so that we could go out for breakfast.

His forehead was jacked up. He had a hickey the size of a walnut. "Jesus! What happened to you?" He touched his head nonchalantly. "Oh played basketball with the boys last night."

Excuse me? Did we not have plans--? He made to step into my apartment. I blocked the entrance. "We had a date last night."

"Oh baby, I'm sorry. Something came up, it was kind of spur of the moment."

"Cell Phone?"

"I'm sorry, baby. It just slipped my mind." I thought about it and shrugged. He exhaled a relieved breath and grinned.

"Call me later," I said while shutting the door in his face.

It felt good to be done with Dean but I still felt mopey, and because of it the rest of the weekend was ruined. I found myself thinking about all the fun I'd had at Club Ritz and how it's always fun when you are hanging with someone who is a friend. Take Tony, for instance. He and I honestly laugh together, unlike with Dean who is not even half as fun. I wished that I could find a guy like Tony; someone who is a friend first and smart, easy to talk to and of course being totally sexy like Tony wouldn't hurt. I guess that skinny Asian girl is having all the fun with him now.

I couldn't wait for Monday. At least I'd have something constructive to do. I saw Tony in the break room and my mood suddenly perked. I sat down next to him.

"Hey, how was your weekend?" I asked.

"Good. Yours?"

"Fine. What'd you do?"

He shrugged. "Nothing much, went to the gym. I hooked up with your cousin and the guys. We played a little basketball-"

"Yeah." I interrupted. "Dean came over with a walnut sized hickey." Tony's lip curled in a peculiar way that wasn't quite a smile. It was really kind of cute, actually.

"How are you and Dean doing?" He asked timidly. I met his eyes and hesitated.

"Fine." I finally answered.

He flexed a muscle in his arm and it was pretty impressive. I couldn't help myself by giving him the once over. Tony is a cutie pie. His hair is cut into a choppy, unruly hairdo that only an expensive barber can make look so good. His body was chiselled and hard, even more so from living in the gym lately. Sometimes I have a hard time taking my eyes from his. His almond shaped, brown eyes reminded me of warm chocolate. I have to admit that there are times where I wanted to touch where his eyelids didn't exist, and then touch where mine did. We were so different physically but I sometimes forget because on the inside we are very much alike.

The next day I put aside my usual heels and dug out a pair of flats. I put on a linen pants suit and clipped on my afro puff ponytail. When I stood next to Tony I revelled at the fact that he was only about an inch and a half, maybe two inches shorter than me, which made him about 5'8"! Hell, I was on an easy six feet in heels. Maybe I'd give them a rest for a while.

Jackie came up to me at the copy machine. "Have you been noticing how good-looking Tony's been getting lately? I mean he was handsome before but now he's VAVOOM!"

I laughed, uncomfortable. I knew Tony liked black women ... and obviously his Asian girlfriend. But would he ever go out with someone like Jackie? She was the whitest woman in the world.

"You're friends with him do you know if he's seeing anyone?"

"Uh, well I've seen a woman driving his car."

"Really? The Jag? It must be serious." Jackie went back to her copying and I realized that I was jealous.

TONY

Playing basketball with the fellas was the first time I got out of my funk in weeks, especially when I went up for a lay-up and my elbow went down hard on Dean's head.

"Oh my bad, man." I said casually. He was hip to me and I didn't get to jack his nuts with my knee. But still it was a good day.

NIKKI

Dean has been blowing up my phone. I don't know why he's been pressing me after three weeks of mediocre sex. Most times I won't even answer the phone, and the one time I did he ended up saying, "So you want to break up with me?"

"Fool, we weren't together in the first place!"

"You fucking T-baby?" I slammed the phone on him. Crazy, stalking, mutha-fucker! From being stressed my neck and shoulders were in knots.

In my office I crossed my arms and rubbed my neck, eyes closed in concentration.

"What's wrong?" Tony was frowning at me. I jumped and he held up his hands. "Sorry your door was opened."

I sighed and relaxed. "Stressed out."

Tony put my cases on my desk. "Over what?"

"Tony," I admitted. "Dean has been stalking me."

"What?" His eyes narrowed.

"I haven't seen him in weeks. But he won't stop calling me. Truth be known, I didn't even think that he was all that into me in the first place—but since I was the one who put on the breaks it's like his ego can't take it."

Tony stared at me intently his fist clenching and unclenching. Finally he took in a shaky voice. He smiled at me. "I'm sure it'll be okay. Dean is a nut but he's not completely crazy."

He gestured to my shoulders. "May I?" I shrugged and immediately winced at the movement. "Sure."

He moved behind me and gently rubbed my neck and shoulders. My eyes closed again, this was heaven. Abruptly he stopped. I tried to glance at him over my shoulder but my tight muscles stopped me.

He sighed. "I'm a licensed massage therapist." I gave him an open mouthed look but he just held up his hand. "I know. I'm a jack of all trades. Look Nikki, you're wound too tight. I can get you loosened up no problem but it would take longer than two minutes in your office.

"What I'll do is come over to your place tonight after work. And then I'll rub the kinks out of your neck and back." He said it so matter-of-factly that I just nodded my head, stunned. He left the office closing the door after him. Now that was strange; my supervisor coming to my house to give me a massage. But Tony is more than that, he's my friend and he happens to have a girlfriend so I guess I was cool with it--although deep down … I'll admit to having a jitter of excitement at the thought of Tony touching me.

After work I was nervous. I showered and changed into sweats, then shorts, and then finally a t-shirt and khakis I mean, what does one wear when getting a massage by ones supervisor-slash-friend?

When the doorbell rang I hurried to answer. He was holding a small bottle of massage oil.

"Hey," He said after walking in and admiring my home. "Nice." It was the first time he'd been inside. I have a modest apartment which I've made upscale with nice furnishings.

"Thanks. Would you like a drink?"

"No." He said simply, walking past me and heading towards the bedroom. He glanced over his shoulder at me. "Ready?"

"Yeah, I guess." He seemed impatient so I followed him into the bedroom.

"I need a towel; a bath towel." I handed him one from my bathroom.

"Yeah, now lay on your belly," he said gesturing from where he was standing by my bed. "I need you lying flat."

What the hell am I doing? I thought as I lay down fully dressed. I felt Tony leaning over me as his fingers kneaded my neck and shoulders. I sighed immediately relaxing. Soon his fingers began to rub deeper into the knots and I hummed sleepily. Then his fingers began to play over the straps of my bra.

Absently he pulled them down over my shoulder and rubbed the grooves that the straps had cut into my flesh. He ran the heel of his hands down my spine inch by inch, and when he reached the clasp of my bra, I felt him reach beneath my shirt and quickly unhook it. I held my breath but the heel of his hand continued its journey down my spine and truthfully it felt much better without the confining bra.

Half an hour later my muscles were liquid and I was as close to sleep as one can get and still be conscious.

"Nikki, take off your shirt."

"Huh?" I asked fully awake.

"Take off your shirt." He showed me the bottle of oil. "I don't want to ruin your shirt. And the towel is to cover you."

I sat up slowly and Tony put the towel up to me since my bra was loose across my body and no longer holding my breasts.

I clutched the towel to my chest and stared at him. I was not about to take off my shirt! But he surprised me when he just stared at me right back. Finally, I just felt plain foolish because I was making this into an issue and he wasn't. He's a legal masseuse and they do massage naked skin.

When he knew he'd won the challenge he turned his back giving me a brief moment of privacy to remove my shirt and bra. Then I lay back down and tried to cover my back with the towel. I felt Tony adjust it then he rubbed something fragrant into my shoulders and neck. This time the massage was deeper- almost to the point of being painful. My neck popped and I sucked in a surprised breath, still not moving.

Tony stopped abruptly. "Did that hurt?" His voice sounded husky.

"No." I murmured. "I could never crack my neck or back on my own … felt good."

He slid the towel down and I caught my breath again until I felt more of the silky oil and his firm fingers kneading the knots out of my lower back. "Tony that feels wonderful … " I had to admit.

"Shhh." he whispered.

"But you do this so well." I murmured.

"I did this for a living for several years."

"Really? Why in the world did you stop?"

"Because although there is potential to make good money, nobody takes this career path seriously. Now relax. Your back is still in knots." Firmly he pressed his thumbs into the dimples right at the swell of my buttocks just beneath my belt.

He paused again and I heard him crack his knuckles, then he focused on where my lower back curved up to my butt. I felt him move the towel and lay it across my butt. Then quickly he slid his hand beneath me and just as he had unfastened the bra he undid the button on my pants and efficiently folded it down a bit until I was exposed to the crack of my ass.

I folded my arms underneath my head and lazily watched him work. In the back of my mind, now that I was completely relaxed, I wondered rather selfishly why I'd known him all these months and I was just now getting a massage.

"Who massages the masseuse?" I asked sleepily.

Tony chuckled. "Unless Wu-tang gets fingers, nobody."

"Not even your girlfriend?" He looked confused.

"Girlfriend? I don't have a girlfriend."

"What about the girl who drives your car sometimes?"

"Oh," he chuckled again. "That's my cousin. She details cars, and was doing some work on mine for me." Well, that mystery was easily solved. Somehow hearing that made me feel even more relaxed.

He ran his fingers up my side and I giggled. "Ticklish?" He smiled when I nodded. "Let me show you something."

He rubbed more oil into his hands then gently stroked my back from neck to ass with his fingertips and nails. I shuddered, my nipples suddenly hardening. It was so tantalizing.

"Feel good?"

I peeked at him; my arms were covered in goose bumps. "I guess." I admitted reluctantly.

He did it again and my clitoris quivered, and I gasped.

"Stop doing that!"

"Sorry," He grinned.

"How ... how'd you know how to do that?"

"Do what?" He asked mischievously.

I rolled my eyes.

"Ancient Chinese secret." He finally spoke.

"But you're not Chinese."

"Ahh, you remembered. Most people think all Asians are the same. That technique I learned from an erotic massage class."

Oh no he did not just lay some erotic touch on me! "Well, Warn me before you do anymore erotic massage!"

He resumed kneading my lower back, yet my clitoris didn't stop quivering.

"Are you still doing it?!" I tried to sit up before remembering I couldn't since I was shirtless.

"No," he replied surprised. "Relax, you're getting tense again, Nikki. Breathe normally." I couldn't. I was horny. I started shaking my foot. He put his hand on my ankle. "Stop."

I inhaled and relaxed but when he started kneading my muscles again I became more turned on than ever.

"It's okay," he whispered, his lips magically right by my ear. "Stop trying to fight it. Let the massage take you where it's going to take you."

I closed my eyes and took Tony's advice to go where the massage was taking me. His fingers moved to the nape of my neck and I groaned. They moved over my shoulder and upper arm and I quivered. They glided over my sides, across the swell of my breasts and my breath got stuck in my chest. There was a soft kiss on my shoulder blade, first one then the other and I sighed.

Then Tony was kissing my neck. Oh god, I wanted to explode right then and there. I turned to him, forgetting about being shirtless and then Tony was kissing me, his mouth hungry over mine as if he had held back for a long time.

As urgent as his kisses were, his powerful hands were gentle as they cradled my face. "Nikki ... " he moaned. I felt him gently thumb my erect nipple. My clitoris, leaped as if there was a direct connection between clit and nipple. It was the most delicious feeling, just his gentle tugging on my nipple and his mouth and tongue on mine.

I pulled back and looked at him. "Tony ... " I was confused. He moved his hand from my nipple to stroke my face. In his eyes I saw something I'd never seen in Dean's or any other man's eye. I could see his need for me. Lightly I let my fingertips glide down his face then across his brow.

He closed his eyes and I touched where his lids should be.

While his eyes were closed I lightly kissed them and he breathed in a surprised breath.

"I've wanted you for so long." His mouth sought out my lips and he kissed me less urgently and more sensually. It was the best damn kiss I'd ever had!

Then there was bamming on the door and I could hear someone yelling outside.

"T-baby! I know you're in there! T-baby!"

"Dean!" I said leaping to my feet. Tony stood trying to adjust the bulge in his pants. He cursed, and then hurried from the bedroom.

"Tony! What are you going to do?" He ignored me and I quickly pulled on my shirt, no time to bother with the bra.

TONY

After all these months I was finally living my fantasy. To be able to put my hands on Nikki's body, to freely explore the silkiness of her skin, the fullness that a masseuse likes to feel in a client—not bones beneath skin. No, I hadn't planned the erotic massage. All I'd wanted to do was to work the knots out of her muscles … and yeah … to touch her.

I did not expect to be kissing her and I was totally blown away when she kissed me back. Then Dean showed up, right when it was getting heated. Nikki didn't want me to do anything, which left me confused. Did she still have feelings for Dean? Did she think I could not protect or defend myself? I opened the front door where Dean was angrily pounding on it.

"What the hell are you doing? This is a residential district- not some strip club!"

Dean pointed to the driveway. "I saw your car; I knew you were fucking her!"

For a minute I was struck dumb. "Man, you're drunk!" He smelled like a distillery.

"Fuck that bitch then!" I punched him in the mouth and before he hit the ground I was on top of him slamming him into the grass with a fistful of his shirt in my hands. I was enraged, enraged that he could be so disrespectful!

"I told you at the club how I felt about Nikki and you went for her anyway. Now you want to call her out of her name?!"

I slammed him angrily again. "Well she's with me now! The knot I put on your head ain't nothing compared to the one I'll put in your ass if you come back around here again!"

He pushed my hands away weakly. "Shit, Tony."

I climbed off him and he lay there rubbing his chin.

I was about to walk away but then stopped. "Why'd you do that, man? I thought we were friends?"

He sat up slowly and then laughed bitterly. "In high school all the bitches wanted to get with you. I don't know how many of them hoes kept coming up to me for me to introduce them to you. Fuck that! I kept all them hoes for myself, and the ones that didn't get with me, I told them your moms would call them names in Japanese!"

My eyes were wide. Dean had been blocking?

I couldn't help it, I just started to chuckle. This fool was for real?

"Well you weren't lying about my moms. She called you names all the time." I shook my head. "I can't believe you man. You're doing this over something that happened in high school?"

He looked at me warily. "You ain't mad?" I offered him a hand up and he took it.

"Not about things that happened when we were sixteen. But the fact that you're still doing it … that's different. Look, it wasn't easy for me fitting in. I didn't look like anybody else-"

"And that's why everybody liked you!"

"And everybody liked you, too. I can't believe you actually begrudged me a little popularity." I narrowed my eyes. "So which girl did you have a crush on that didn't give you the time of day because she wanted me?" Dean's mouth opened then closed.

"Amy." My eyes bugged. "Amy? That skinny white girl that dumped me for Pooh?" I bent over and roared in laughter. "All those fine sistas in school and you had it for Amy?" Tears streamed down my cheeks. Dean stalked away angrily. I turned back to the apartment. Nikki was standing there looking sad. My laughter stopped instantly and I sobered. Her feelings were hurt by what Dean had said.

"I was just a pawn?" I took her arm and led her back into the apartment, practically slamming the door shut after us.

She crossed her arms in front of her and wouldn't meet my eyes.

"It pisses me off that in trying to hurt me he hurt you. I'm sorry you got stuck in the middle of this." I stared at her. "Do you want me to kick his ass?"

She blinked at me. "I think you already did that." Then she smiled. "So you put that lump on his forehead?"

I looked at her sheepishly. "Yeah."

Nikki snickered and walked towards me slowly. She put her arms around me and kissed me. "So I'm with you now, huh?"

I kissed her back.

"As longs as you understand that I'm not in this for the short term. Nikki, I've been attracted to you since the day you walked into the office. That's a long time to want someone."

She gave me a surprised look. "I didn't know … "

"How do you feel about having a Japanese boyfriend?" She raised an unsure eyebrow and I felt my heart sink.

"The Japanese part doesn't concern me … but I've never dated someone so much … uhm, smaller than me-"

I lifted her and swung her effortlessly into my arms. She whooped and clutched me tightly as if she was surprised that I could lift her so effortlessly.

"Tony!!"

"Nikki, trust me." I carried her into the bedroom and kicked the door shut.

NIKKI

Dean is an asshole and a child. But I'm happy that it turned out that way because now I can focus on my attraction for Tony and recognize it for what it is. I want him. I want him as my friend, I want him as my man and most of all I want him as my lover.

He carried me into the bedroom as if I weighed nothing. I stared into his chocolate eyes searching for … I don't know. But what I saw was his desire for me and it sent my heart racing.

He placed me on my bed and I didn't budge as he began to slowly undress. My brain was going, 'Oh my God,' and my breath was tight in my chest when I saw the cut of his muscles. I knew that he was fit and toned but having never seen him out of his shirt I was blown away by his six pack. He looked amazing!

When he slipped off his pants, I didn't know what to focus on more; the bulge in his boxer briefs or the smoky look that he held in his narrowed eyes. I decided on his thick cock because I can look into his eyes any day, but I wanted his cock. Mmm, my mouth was watering because I am so oral. I reached out and Tony put his hand over mine and guided it to him. He wrapped my fingers around his thickness and I was lost.

"What do you want?" He asked.

"Your cock in my mouth." Then I covered my mouth with my free hand, shocked at my words. Tony just looked at me seriously.

"Good girl. Because I want your pussy in mine." Then he grinned and it was so sexy. It was as if he was saying, 'See, I knew we would be in synch.'

He climbed onto the bed and finished undressing me, not allowing me to help. When I was down to my hot pink boy shorts he watched me. My skin tingled everywhere that his eyes looked. My nipples tightened, my stomach quivered and then he gently pushed my thighs apart, as if he had every right to feast between them.

His fingers drew down my panties and when they were lying on the floor his eyes stared down at my slit. He was so quiet but I could see something like awe in his look and I knew it was an expression that he wasn't aware that he wore. Then I knew that I had been a fool to overlook this man.

He lowered his mouth to my mound and kissed my nether lips. My body began to tremble and he hadn't really done anything. I just knew that I needed that touch. No, not just the touch; I needed someone to want me in the way that he apparently did. His tongue came out and I felt him trace my opening. While I like having a man eat me, it's not the thing that I consider a 'must' have. But in that moment the sensation of his tongue on my pussy nearly made me explode and it had just been two seconds!

His fingers spread me and then his tongue was probing back and forth and all around. I heard myself making noises that I'd never heard myself making before. His tongue nudged and teased my clit and then when I thought I'd go crazy he jackhammered his tongue right on my clit! My back arched and I sucked in a sharp breath. Immediately he began lapping and sucking, alternating between gentle and rough in such a way that it took my breath away!

His strong hands held me in place but when my body started to quiver I sat up breathlessly, not wanting it to end as quickly as it was about to. "My turn." He looked up with bleary eyes and expression that was like, 'Oh sorry I forgot you were still there'. It was so cute that I giggled. I don't giggle, but this time I did. Oh, yeah … my turn.

I pushed him over until he was on his back and he scooted up in bed and held a slight smile on his face as he looked down the length of his body at me. I was just dazed by the sight of his dick as it stood straining straight in the air. The only dicks I'm familiar with are the ones attached to black men. I guess I thought an Asian dick would be short and pink. On the contrary, Tony's dick was fat and brown and I almost spoke what I was thinking, 'You have a black man's dick!' Even though my mouth watered for it, I took a moment to appraise his body. His torso was completely hairless, so the thatch of black hair that sprouted between his thighs was a shocking contrast. I reached out finally and stroked his rock hard shaft. His eyes twinkled and he looked as pleased as if I'd just given him a blowjob.

The color of his scrotum was darker than the rest of him. Damn, I couldn't wait to put that thing in my mouth. First I kissed up and down his length, teasing his balls with my tongue. His dick lurched at my touch and Tony groaned audibly. Good, he was a moaner. I loved moaners.

I gently pulled one and than the other testicle into my mouth and Tony gasped and dropped his head onto the bed, eyes rolled up into the top of his head. I love a dick in my mouth and especially when the owner loves being sucked. I teased his head and massaged his shaft before finally lowering my mouth over him and deep throating him.

"Nikki!" He yelled, moments before pumping in and out of my mouth frantically. I opened my throat and let him fuck my mouth until the sweet/salty taste of his precum flooded my senses and threatened to send me into my own oblivion.

"I'm going to cum ... " He warned, but I didn't care. I wanted him to spill himself into my mouth. With a last wail of pleasure, I felt his first creamy spurts shoot down my throat. I kept sucking wetly until he reached over and urged me over onto my back again. Quickly he moved between my thighs again.

"Come on baby ... " He mumbled as he worked my pussy with his tongue, mouth and teeth. When I felt his finger slip inside of me, my body spasmed, and with a yell I climaxed roughly while he verbally and physically encouraged me.

"Tony ... " I purred when I could finally speak.

47

"Hmmm?" He had gathered me into his arms and I was like liquid.

"How do you say happy in Japanese?"

"Ureshii."

"Ureshii." I repeated.

He closed his arms around me and nodded in agreement. "Totemo ureshii yo." He yawned. "I am so happy." When I looked up at him, he had that sexy smile back on his lips and his eyes were closed in contentment.

PART II

In the sky, there is no distinction of east and west; people create distinctions out of their own minds and then believe them to be true.
-Buddha

NIKKI

I have been dating Toi Yakamoto for two weeks now. Most people that see us together probably couldn't conceive that we're an item. I mean, look at me. I'm 5'10", I weigh two ... I'm a size ... I'm voluptuous, let's put it that way.

I have a penchant for the extravagant. Yes, I like my weaves, my long ponytails and afro puffs and extensions. And God gave cleavage and I like to show it! I'm fine; I know it and I don't have any problems saying it. People have called me Queen Latifah since I was a teenager.

Now Toi, or Tony to his friends, is 5'7'... 5'8" stretching it. He's transformed his genetically slight Asian body to a well-toned, muscled one. The Japanese ends there. When he opens his mouth he sounds like a straight up brother!

He listens to R&B, grew up in the hood, dates black women, drives a Jag and knows how to give a mean massage. When he was growing up his nickname was T-baby of all things!

Appearance-wise, we couldn't be more opposite. But where it counts T and I have lots in common---he could be my soul mate. But you want to know the jacked up thing about our relationship? T is afraid to introduce me to his Mama.

TONY

Nikki thinks I'm scared of my mom ... which I guess she has to believe, the alternative being that I'm ashamed of her. Neither could be further from the truth. I have one reason for not wanting to introduce them to each other. I love them both.

My mother is not going to like Nikki and Nikki is not going to like that my mom doesn't like her. Then they'll want me to choose and I don't want to be put in that situation. If you're saying to yourself, you're a grown man and your mama needs to stay out of your personal business, then you obviously are not Asian. Perhaps if you are Jewish you will get an idea of my plight — otherwise, just shut up.

Asian mothers cannot be disowned; they cannot mind their own business, for their child is their business ... and they guilt. My mom is very important to me but she has never been close to changing me, though not from lack of trying. Truthfully, if I can get both of them wrapped around the idea of each other before they meet then it might not be Armageddon! Here it goes...

I go to my parent's house for dinner every Sunday. It wasn't any type of religious gathering, my parents are Buddhists, but Sunday is just the least busy day on anyone's schedule. Every Sunday we

51

have a traditional Japanese meal. Usually it is a nabe, which is a hot pot that mom sits on the table and you add meats, vegetables, or seafood. Like sukiyaki-that's a nabe dish.

This Sunday we also had Tonkatsu, deep fried pork cutlets over cabbage and tea cakes for dessert.

"Oa-dkei-teowshii-desu," Mom said, giving me a kiss and squeezing my cheeks.

"Hi, Mom. Where's dad?"

"He's in the garden trying to salvage some tomatoes."

"Dinner smells good." I stopped in my tracks. Sitting on the couch was a chubby Asian woman with a broad smile. I gave mom a sideways glance and tried to hide my exasperation.

She was always springing a blind date on me! "Toi, this Sumi Sikora," Sumi stood up demurely and offered her hand.

"Hajimemashite."

"Konnichiwa." I responded. "Eigo wo hanashi-masu-ra?" I had asked her in broken Japanese if she spoke English.

"Yes."

"Good, my Japanese is very poor."

Mom ushered me to sit down by Sumi. "Toi, please keep Sumi company while I finish dinner. I'll bring you semkei and tea." She disappeared into the kitchen.

I gave Sumi an uncomfortable look. "So ... how do you know my mom?"

"I … don't know your mom. I've never met her before today. My grandmother works at an Asian food market and your mother came through her aisle. She said you were looking for an Asian wife-"

"What!?" That was the last straw. I have to put a stop to this.

"Toi," Sumi said hastily when I jumped up. "My grandmother does this kind of thing to me all the time. When I told her I didn't want to come she went on and on until … honestly, I'd rather sit here and be uncomfortable than listen to my grandmother's mouth." I relaxed. After a moment I sat down too.

"My mom does this to me all the time, too."

"Toi, I have to be honest with you-"

"Please, call me Tony. Honest about what?"

"I hate Japanese food. I'm scared to death that your mother might serve eel, and I don't want to offend her." I laughed. I liked Sumi. My mom mysteriously stayed away and Sumi and I had a good conversation. But I still had a mission and nothing was keeping me from it.

"You know Sumi, you seem like a nice person but … I was coming today to tell my parents that I had met someone special." Sumi gave me a speculative look.

"She must not be Asian."

"No, she's not.

"Then you're very brave. Maybe it's good that I am here so that your parents will be on their best behavior." I smiled. Excellent.

At dinner my mom looked so pleased that we all were getting along comfortably. There was no eel on the table so Sumi oohed and aahed and seemed to show genuine appreciation for the dishes.

"Toi works at a big American Real-Estate office. He supervisor there ... make big buck, have good benefits." Mom said to Sumi.

"Mom," my face turned red. "You sound like you're trying to sell me to the highest bidder."

"What?" she asked, feigning confusion. "You not big shot? You make decision, hire and fire-"

"No. I don't hire and fire."

Mom smiled at Sumi. "Gomen. My son is ... how you say modest. Have some Nabe." Dad winked at me silently as I pressed my lips together. Well here it goes. I looked at Sumi who seemed to silently encourage me.

"So ... " I began, "I saw a very funny movie just last week with Nikki. It had that actor that I like in it, mom-"

"Nikki?" She interrupted. "Who's Nikki?"

"Nikki's a girl I've been seeing for the last few weeks."

"Nikki," Mom said thoughtfully. "That Asian name?" Sumi looked down nervously. I swallowed.

"No. She not Asian."

"Not even Korean?"

"No."

"How about Hawaiian?"

"She's not Asian at all ... she's not even white." Mom looked relieved, but only for a moment.

"What mean 'She not white?' Not French I hope."

"Nikki's … black." Mom and dad looked at me perplexed.

"What mean? Kuro?" They looked at each other in confusion.

"Not Kuro." Which was the color black.

"Koko-jin." This roughly translated to Negro. Mom gasped, dropping her chopsticks. Sumi stood up suddenly.

"I'm a lesbian. I know you probably don't care because you don't know me. But," she glanced at me, "if Tony's brave enough to tell his family he's dating a black girl, then I'm going to tell my parents I'm gay."

My father looked at me. "What's … lesbian?"

"Okama," I said. My mother fainted.

When I got to Nikki's she was playing some old Jazz; Grover Washington, Jr., I think. She had stripped down to a sheer negligee panties and chemise. When I saw the dark brown of her areolas through the pink material it took all my resolve not to suck them through the cloth!

"Hi baby." She wrapped her arms around my neck and gave me a sensuous kiss. Kicking the door shut, I returned the kiss, gripping her ample ass in the palms of my hands. She loved the fact that even though I was technically smaller than her, I could carry her with ease and she wrapped her juicy legs around my waist.

I walked us into the living room, tonguing her mouth and throat. "T … " she groaned.

"Mmmm." I sat us down in her oversized reclining chair with her knees straddling me.

Then I could release her ass and finally reach for her breasts. She pushed the chair back into the reclining position and began grinding her pelvis into mine. I was already rock hard. "Nikki ... "

I groaned and pushed the strap of her top down over her shoulders until her beautiful brown breasts fell out of the sheer fabric. But she wouldn't let me taste. She just pushed me back into the chair and reached between us to undo the zipper of my pants. Sensing how she wanted it, I pushed the crotch of her panties to the side. She was so wet my fingertips came away damp! She shuddered and roughly gripped me and guided me into her hot pussy. Then, she proceeded to ride me like she was in a rodeo! It was rough and fast. And after we both climaxed I gripped her and allowed us to gently tumble to the carpeted floor.

"I've been wanting to do that all day," she panted. I sat up on my elbow and watched her.

"Me too. Sorry I had to leave-"

"No, it's cool. Sunday is your day with your parents. How was dinner?"

I glanced away. "Delicious. My mom made these crackers-"

"I mean did you tell them about me?"

"Oh." I stood up and straightened my clothes. "Yeah. I told them." I could sense her watching me even though I was preoccupied with re-zipping my pants.

"And?"

I had been trying to think of the right way to describe dinner on the drive over to Nikki's place. I'd even contemplated lying ... but that wasn't a good way to start, what I hoped would be a long-term relationship.

"She fainted." I mumbled.

"What?"

I sighed. "My mom fainted. But ... " I added when her eyes got big. "It could have been because Sumi announced she was a lesbian."

"Who is Sumi?" Oh shit ... maybe I shouldn't have mentioned Sumi.

"That would be the blind date that my mom had set up for me."

Nikki just sat quietly on the floor and I didn't have the guts to open my mouth.

"I see that I have my work cut out for me," she finally said with a determined glint in her eyes.

NIKKI

I ain't going to lie. T's mama fainting when she found out that her son was dating a black woman kinda pissed me off, but then I put things into perspective. For instance, she didn't know me. It wasn't personal ... yet.

Now when I told my people about Tony, I started with my cousin Jay since T and Jay had grown up together. I remembered how Jay had warned me that T liked black girls with big asses and big titties—which happened to be two of my best attributes. And I remembered how I told Jay that there was no way anything was happening between us—not only because of the race thing, but T was also my boss!

And now look at us. And my cousin didn't let me down. He broke down to my family how cool Tony is, and other than the initial tentative "What the hell are you thinking?!" from my father, no one gave me a hard time. Well, actually my friend Tabby had the nerve to ask me if Asians have smaller penises.

Tony's dick keeps me more than happy and I have no complaints in that department.

Anyway, I was taught to never give a girlfriend too much info about your man so I've never told anyone this, but Tony is the best in the bedroom. The first time we ever did it was after he beat up my ex. I didn't even know Tony liked me like that. He came to my place to give me a massage and we ended up making out.

He asked me how I felt about dating a Japanese guy and I was honest. The Japanese part didn't bother me—but I'm a big woman and I've always needed a big guy to make me feel secure. He picked me up like I was a rag doll. I could feel his steely muscles as he cradled me in his arms. Trust me, he said. And I have, every since.

That night I realized that I could say and do whatever I wanted in bed with Tony. More times than not it was hard and fast. I asked him once to spank me, never having experienced it before. He surprised me by not hemming and hawing. He never said "I can't hit you, Nikki." He just flipped me over, smacked my ass sharply until it stung deliciously and I climaxed just from his hand repeatedly striking my bare bottom.

Yeah, the sex is great, but beyond that Tony is just fun to be with. With him it's not just dinner and a movie. We've been out dancing, listening to light Jazz, walking in the park. I don't know how much longer we're going to be able to work together without tipping everyone off to our relationship.

No, we're not getting freaky at work. But it's difficult to even look at him without it getting heated. And he constantly puts his hands on me whether it's to graze my shoulders with his fingers when leaning over my chair, or to brush my hand when passing me new cases. The only thing … the only thing … is

Tony's   Mama.

TONY

I called my Mom Monday from work. I know, I know, I know. Drama, guilt, whatever. But if your mom is affected so greatly about something that she has to faint, maybe it's worth talking about.

"Mom? How are you feeling?"

"Oh ... Geki-desu." She sighed. I'm fine.

"I sent leftovers home with Sumi. Her poor parents. She never find husband, have children, if like other girls."

"Actually it's not uncommon for gays and lesbians to adopt."

"Maybe. Times change. Hard to keep up," she sighed. There was a quality to her voice that let me know she was genuine.

"Mom. How do you feel about Nikki and me?"

"Nikki? Who Nikki? Oh, your friend. Why should I care who you chose as friend? Have lesbian, have black friend, I don't care." I leaned back in my office chair.

"Nikki is more than my friend."

"What? You married to this girl?"

"No-"

"K-ni-shinai-de!" She brushed me off with a never mind. "I put your father on phone. You speak to him." Then she was gone.

Dad came on the line after a moment. We talked for a few. He never brought up the subject of Nikki and neither did I.

"Tony. You're quiet. What's wrong?" Nikki asked me later at lunch. I smiled.

"I'm okay." I briefly touched her hand on the table. I didn't see any co-workers in the restaurant but you can never be too careful.

"You look tense. I think I might need to come over and give you a massage." She said in a seductive low voice. My mouth went dry. That's one thing we've never done;,me on the receiving end of a massage.

"I don't know. Wu-tang may get jealous. I promised her that I would never let another woman rub on my back."

"Well, me and Wu-tang have an agreement. She lets me rub on you and I promise to keep my eyes open for a nice Siberian Husky." She sipped her tea then leaned back in her chair casually.

"Tony," She said demurely. "Would you like to talk dirty to me?"

I licked my lips then smiled. I leaned back in my own chair then sipped my own tea absently as if we were having a casual conversation.

"Right now, baby, my cock is so hard; I could go back to the office and jerk off to the thought of you, just like I used to every night before we got together." Her breath came in a rush.

"Better yet. I think I'll keep it hard and walk in and out of your office letting you see what you do to me." Nikki's eyes fluttered, her breathing strained. She tapped her feet then crossed her gorgeous legs. I knew she was squeezing her pussy lips together.

"Your pussy's wet, isn't it?" I asked in a barely audible whisper. Nikki closed her eyes. I saw her hands grip the arms of her chair. Then she looked at me with hooded eyes.

"Yes."

"We can't have that ... you walking around all day with a wet pussy. I guess I'll have to get you back in the bathrooms, pull off those wet panties and lick every drop of you down my throat."

"Oh! She groaned and I saw her shudder, her breath coming in quick spurts. Then it was like the movie; When Harry met Sally, but quieter. She had the quietest orgasm I'd ever seen because my baby is usually loud!

When she was finished, I was the one sweating. Demurely, she picked up her tea and sipped, giving me an innocent smile. I shifted in my seat.

"What's the matter baby? You need me to stroke you off under the table?"

"Nikki," I warned. "I'll have to go home and change if you make me cum."

"Who're you telling? I'm sitting here in my own wet spot."

Well, I couldn't have my baby walking in the office with a tell-tale wet spot or me with a tell-tale erection. I made up some errand for us to run, took her back to my place, removed her panties, then I licked her pussy dry.

NIKKI

Sunday Tony went to his parents for diner again. I know that I shouldn't be concerned but I can't stop wondering who she is trying to set him up with this time. I felt like bum rushing it ... hey, that wasn't a bad idea. I called up Tony on his cell while he was with his parents.

"Hello, Nikki? Everything okay?" His voice was anxious with concern.

"Yeah T-baby. Y'all eating yet?"

"No. Why?"

"T, I thought maybe your mom would get me better if she actually met me."

"Maybe—Nikki ... I do want you to meet my folks, but this is not the right time."

"Humph." I said disappointed.

"Baby, I'll come over after dinner. Okay?"

"Okay." I hung up stinging. T had never told me no before. It definitely smarted. Why play games? I mean, after all, I'm his woman. It felt to me like times when things would be going well in a relationship and then you met the friends or family and things got cold. Maybe they had said I was too fat, or too ghetto, I don't know. But friends and family went a long way to influencing a relationship.

I made myself a drink. I couldn't shake a creeping sadness.

TONY

Mom looked at me sideways. She had heard my one-sided conversation with Nikki. Broken English or not she knew what was going down. They were two powerful women. Nikki knew about mom, now mom was suspecting about Nikki.

When I got to Nikki's place she was already in bed. An empty wine glass sat on her otherwise neat side table. I leaned over and kissed her.

"Hi baby. You're in bed early." She looked at me.

"How was dinner?"

"Good. I'm sorry about not inviting you. It's just that-"

"Don't worry about it. I'll meet them when I meet them."

She turned back around and snuggled into her pillow. I sat on the bed and put my hand on her back.

"Nothing would make me happier than for you to meet my folks Nikki. But I know my mother. All she wants is for me to settle down with a nice Asian girl. It doesn't matter what I want. It's just that tradition is all she knows."

Nikki didn't move. With a sigh I stood up. "I'm a pretty big disappointment to my Mom. I'm not the son that followed the old ways. I don't talk like her or appreciate the same things she does. I'm haku-jin. A westerner."

"Didn't they come to America for a better life?" She asked without turning around.

"Yes." She rolled over and looked at me with sad eyes.

"Then they succeeded, because you are living The American Dream. If they wanted you to be like them then maybe they should have stayed in Japan and raised you in a Japanese culture instead of raising you in an American one and expecting you to emulate a culture you weren't even in."

I couldn't speak. It was so true ... and so false. I had a lot of Japanese influences. We were involved in a lot of cultural activities and were part of a large Asian community from temple to clubs. I knew a lot of beautiful Asian girls and have met Asian boys to befriend.

But it was me that rejected it. I engulfed the hip-hop world and that wouldn't allow me to be untrue to what was in my heart. So honestly, it's not just my Mom that guilts me. I have enough guilt of my own for rejecting my race.

I fidgeted and Nikki finally lay back on her pillow. "I guess ... I'll go home." I kissed her cheek and she didn't move. "See you at work." I went home and slept alone in my bed for the first time in weeks.

NIKKI

I've allowed myself to get too close to Tony too fast. Not knowing how this is going to end up, I've decided to move back a bit. It hurts to even think about it, but I've been devastated by a relationship before and it wasn't nearly as deep and meaningful as this one. I missed him so much after he left my apartment, that I barely slept a wink. The next day at work Tony was in conference for most of the day.

I had lunch with some of my co-workers, my thoughts on him completely.

"Nikki? Earth to Nikki?" Lisa called. The other ladies laughed.

"Oh, I'm sorry, Lisa. What were you saying?" And it had been like that all morning. I had a client whose name I couldn't remember and in the span of fifteen minutes I called her Mrs Banner, Mrs Bennett, and Mrs Benson.

There was a knock at my door later and Tony came into my office, shutting the door after him.

"Hey," he said tentatively.

"Hey."

"Sorry, I haven't been able to see you today until now. It's been a big mess. All middle management has been stuck in meetings."

"Yeah, I know."

"What're you doing tonight?" Quickly, I tried to think of something to say. "Can you come to my place for dinner?" He added. "I'm making a completely Japanese meal---and I've invited my parents. It's time for them to accept who I am---or not. But, if they don't I can't make it my problem."

I just burst out crying. I had no idea that I would be so relieved. Tony hurried to me and took me in his arms.

"Nikki, baby, don't cry! Shh. I'm sorry, baby." He rocked me soothingly.

"No, I'm sorry T-baby. I thought … she was going to make you take a second look at me."

He kissed my tears. "I've already taken a second and third look at you. And I love you-"

"Oh! Excuse me … I didn't—" We both turned to the door. Lisa was standing in the doorway looking like she'd seen a ghost. Tony and I quickly moved away from each other. But it was too late. She's seen him kissing me. And she had to have heard him say that he loved me. Tony loved me …

Lisa quickly hurried out, shutting the door behind her. Tony and I looked at each other. The cat was out of the bag, and with him being my supervisor, it was not going to make it pretty.

I couldn't do much about what Lisa had seen; and besides, I was having dinner with Tony's parents! And he had confessed to loving me! I decided to "arrive" at Tony's instead of lounging around as if it was my place. Besides, it was going to take him some time to complete dinner and I wanted to take that time to make myself presentable.

Finding something conservative in my closet wasn't easy, but I settled on brown slacks, ox blood loafers and a tan button down blouse with three-quarter length wing sleeves. I had a lot of hair to choose from but I decided on a tight bun at the back my neck and simple silver studs in my ears.

I toned down my makeup and when it was all said and done, I looked in the mirror and hated everything I saw. I took out the hair and pulled off the clothes and kicked off the loafers. I put on a long rust colored swing out skirt that hugged my hips snuggly then flared at my knees, taupe stockings and gold and rust heels. The blouse I chose was a pale chemise with demure cleavage that complimented the rust of the skirt. Over this went the rust colored jacket that ran over my hips and hugged them nicely when buttoned, though I chose to wear it loose.

To finish the ensemble I put on amber dangling earrings and matching necklace. The hair that looked best with the outfit was a two toned fall that flowed past my shoulders into layers of ringlets. By the time I'd gotten re-dressed I was running a bit behind. It looked like I'd truly be making an entrance.

TONY

Dinner was at eight so that meant I didn't have much time to shop and prepare the meal. I was going to do sushi, which meant I had to run to the fish market for sushi quality fish. I knew Nikki would like some tempura veggies, and to round it off would be an entrée of eel and tea rice. I wasn't worried about serving eel to Nikki. My baby was down for new experiences. My Mom loved a good soup, so I decided on a quick egg drop. I put some soothing jazz on the sound system and drank warmed Saki.

I found myself actually looking forward to gathering all my favorite people in the world in one room. I showered quickly and changed into black slacks and a cream sweater with the sleeves pushed up to my elbows. The doorbell rang.

Anxiously I answered it. I was hoping it would be Nikki first but it was Mom and Dad. I hugged and kissed them.

"Come on in."

"Mmm." Mom said, handing me her jacket, "Smell good."

"I'm going to the restroom." Dad said. "Get me a glass of ice water, son."

Mom followed me into the kitchen. "I set table."

"It's already set. You want something to drink? Water, juice, Saki?"

"Tea." I made us both a cup of tea and took it to the living room on a tray where Dad joined us. Mom bit into an almond cookie.

"You bake?"

"Hai. It's your recipe."

She nodded. "Did good."

"So where is your friend?" Dad asked. Mom gave him the evil eye. He shrugged. Mom's game was that if she pretended Nikki didn't exist, I'd know how little she thought of it.

"She'll be here shortly." No sooner were the words out of my mouth before the doorbell rang again.

"That's her." I leaped up and answered the door. Before she could come in I gripped her and kissed her quickly.

"Hi. You look great. Come in." She did look great. With a shaky sigh she stepped into the lion's den.

"Mom, Dad," they stood up. "This is Nikita Mason; my girlfriend. And Nikki, this is my Mom Kayo and my father, Morio Yakamoto."

"Nice to meet you." Dad spoke, extending his hand to her

"O-ai deki-ti ureshii desu." Nikki responded, surprising us all.

"Ahh." My Dad smiled. "You speak a little Japanese."

"Just what Tony has taught me."

"Sit down everyone." I said. "Nikki, do you want something to drink?"

She looked at the table at what everyone else was drinking.

"Tea would be good."

I hurried to the kitchen hoping nothing would go wrong in the short time that I would be gone. Nikki liked her tea slightly sweetened, so I made it up quickly and went back to the living room. They all looked up when I walked in.

"What're you talking about?"

"We didn't know you and Nikki worked together," Dad said.

"Yes." I handed Nikki her tea and sat down beside her. "We've been working in the same office about six months, dating about one month."

"You not have problem having friend at work in same office?" Mom asked me. She gave Nikki a brief smile, because my mom would never be intentionally rude. That would be low class.

"Well, there hasn't been a problem yet." I said honestly.

"You not rock boat, Toi." Mom said passionately. She sighed and looked at Nikki. "How your family feel about you date Japanese man?"

Nikki sighed too. "My family trusts my judgment."

"Ge-ge?" She asked, and then in Japanese she said more to herself, "What do the young know about life with no experience?"

"Eigo-de- itte-kudasai," I said softly. Please speak English. My mother leaned forward.

"Excuse me. You nice lady or my son not care for you. But you two are much different."

Dad put his hand on her knee, and she looked at him briefly then sat back in her seat.

"Not much different- not on the inside." Was Nikki's response.

Mom didn't respond. I had hoped that they could have talked and gotten familiar with each other before this. I stood.

"Why don't we eat?"

Dinner was ultra-polite everyone complimented the food. Nikki seemed to like the eel and conversation was neutral, about nothing personal or sensitive. After dinner we had teacakes and Nikki and I had Saki while Mom and Dad had tea.

"You like Japanese cooking?" Mom asked Nikki.

"Yes. I didn't know much about Japanese cooking before I met Tony, but I've grown to really love it."

"Ahh." My Dad smiled. "Soon you learn to speak broken Japanese well, just like my son." We all laughed.

Mom said, "We should have sent Toi to Japanese academy like planned. Toi want to be like friends, listen to hippity-hop."

Nikki smiled and looked at me. "That's not all he listens to. He introduced me to a Japanese jazz musician Keiko Matsui."

"Jazz? That not Japanese music."

"No, but she fuses jazz and elements of traditional Japanese sounds."

"Humph." Mom huffed. "I no like Jazz."

"You like Kenny G." Dad said. Mom gave him the evil eye.

"We go home now. Nice meet you, Nikki." Mom stood abruptly.

Dad took Nikki's hand as we all stood. "It was nice to meet you Nikki. Tony has never brought a girl home before. We worried that he not like girls but boys."

"Dad! " I laughed. Nikki covered her smile with her other hand.

"It was nice to meet you Mr Yakamoto, Mrs Yakamoto." Mom shook her hand briefly then turned to the door. Suddenly she turned back and looked at Nikki closely. Her brow knitted in an odd way. Nikki self-consciously smoothed her hand over her skirt. Mom looked at me, and then frowned.

"Toi, you bring Nikki to dinner Sunday. Nikki," she turned back still frowning, "you come?" Nikki gave her a perplexed look.

"Yes and thank you. I'd love to come to dinner." We looked at each other, confused. I walked Mom and Dad to their car. When I came back Nikki was dabbing at beads of sweat on her forehead.

"You alright?" I pulled her into my arms. "I think I'm going to need one of your world famous massages after that." I pulled her into my arms and kissed her.

"Done. You did good, baby."

"Yeah." Nikki frowned. "What was up with that last second change of mind?" I shrugged. I was just happy there was one.

NIKKI

Dinner hadn't gone too bad. I was so relieved that it was over, though, and I could move forward with Tony. Tony's Dad seemed very open minded and cool. Mrs Y ... well, I was reserving judgment until after Sunday dinner.

Tony and I both worried about work the next day, with Lisa walking in on us. But Lisa pretended that nothing was at odds, at least around me.

This coming Friday was Sweetest Day and the weekend before, I had slipped away and bought Tony some bling; a platinum watch from Cartier! I had never spent so much on a gift to a man before, but it felt right. I could barely wait for Friday to come!

Wednesday when I walked into the break room some of the ladies had their heads together. When they saw me they suspiciously changed the subject. I guess it was time for Tony and I to start discussing the possibility of unemployment.

That night Tony said that he wanted to take me shopping for Sweetest Day. "Make sure you clear your weekend. I need Friday after work and all day Saturday. You'll need to pack an overnight bag."

"What? We're going away for the weekend?"

"Maybe."

"Well, what should I pack to wear?" He smiled, not giving an inch. "Something comfortable to shop in."

When Friday came we left directly from work. That morning, Tony had taken my bags and placed them in the trunk with his own, and as usual we drove in together. But when we left I didn't see Tony's Jag anywhere. He just smiled at me.

"I made arrangements for my cousin to pick up my car and take it back to my place."

"Why?" He gestured for me to follow him and we walked away from the office and our co-workers until we were two blocks away. We stopped at a restaurant that we regularly frequented. There was a limo waiting for us. I looked at Tony in surprise. The chauffeur got out and opened the door for us.

"Sorry for the walk but I didn't want to give our co-workers any more to gossip about."

We got comfortable. It was a beautiful limo! Tony hit a button and smooth jazz began to play; Boney James, one of my favorites. The sound system was magnificent.

"Thirsty?" He picked up a bottle of Cristal that was on ice. I nodded, smiling. He poured us each a glass full. We clinked. "Let's toast," he said, "to love."

My heart swelled. "To love."

Tony kissed me then we sipped the best wine I'd ever had in my life. There was a bowl full of the biggest strawberries. He fed me one. I bit into it like I was biting into a peach. It was so sweet!

"T-baby." I chuckled. "Who knew you had so much class?" He put the strawberry down and set our glasses on the mini bar. He was no longer smiling as he moved to sit next to me on the overstuffed leather seat. I watched him, confused.

"Nikki ... " He kissed me. My eyes fluttered shut his lips trailed down my neck and past the hollow of my ear. "Nikki ... " he murmured. I felt his hand slip into my blouse and cup my breast.

His fingers sought my nipple and gently squeezed. I sighed and ran my hands through his silky spiked hair. He unbuttoned my blouse and smoothly dropped to his knees before me. He pushed just enough of my breasts out of my bra until my nipple peeked out of the lacy black material.

Then I felt his mouth cover it. I groaned as he softly sucked and lapped first one then the other.

"T-baby ... " I spread my legs as he hiked my skirt up over my hips. Then I wrapped them around him. He released my nipple and plunged his tongue into my mouth groaning against my lips as he pulled my hips forward off the seat and against his pelvis.

We spent the next several minutes just kissing. Oh, I loved his lips and tongue! I reached between us and unzipped him. Being on the pill we made the mutual decision long ago to forgo condoms. So when his cock entered me, straining against my most sensitive parts, I couldn't help but yell out.

Tony pumped into me, burying his face into my neck and sounding like he was sobbing. I unclasped my legs as the feeling intensified. And don't ask me how but I brought my knees up and Tony pushed them up over his shoulder where the pumping of his hips slowed until he was just pressing and rotating against me; pelvis to pelvis.

He raised his face from my neck and he watched me with red, glassy eyes. He noted every reaction to each thrust, each stroke. Finally I couldn't hold it back any longer and the next thrust pushed me to the brink and the one after that over the edge. I cried out throwing my head from side to side.

Tony lowered my legs, watching me until he went over himself, crying out, blinking and sucking his breath.

"I'm in love with you, Nikki!" I heard him whimper. "I love you." He said much quieter. He put his head back into the crook of my neck. "I love you so much." He sighed.

With hooded eyes I pulled his head back and looked into his moist ones. I cradled his face allowing my fingers to stroke his eyelashes, his lips, his jaw. "I love you." I closed my eyes and murmured. "I love you … I'm in love with you-" He hugged me taking my breath away.

After a while I heard him murmur. "The limo's slowing down we better fix ourselves."

"Oh shit!" I pushed him off me and tucked and pushed body parts back into my clothing. Since T's look was dishevelled, yet corporate casual, all he had to do was pull his hands through his hair and fasten his pants. I had to find tissues to clean away our sex, fix my wig, and re-apply my lipstick. A spritz of perfume hopefully hid the evidence of our love-making. Tony was watching me with a smirk.

I gave him a worried look. "Do you think the chauffeur's going to know what we were doing back here?"

"With the way you were yelling? Yeah."

"Oh my God!" I said, mortified.

"Baby, it's not anything he hasn't heard before." He handed me a fresh glass of Cristal and we drank quietly listening to music and eating strawberries until the driver announced over an intercom that we had arrived.

Through the tinted windows I saw that we were at the airport. I looked at Tony surprised.

"We're at the airport, T!"

"What?!" He exclaimed. "I told him to take us to the bus station!"

I rolled my eyes and then we both laughed. When the driver opened the door, he kept a blank, but polite face. Of course, I was positive that he had kept the intercom on and had been listening to every moan! I glanced to see if he had a tell-tale erection. He didn't.

T would not tell me where we were going until we got to our terminal and I could see for myself that were on our way to New York; Manhattan.

My eyes got big. "You're taking me shopping in New York?!" I squealed and gripped his arm. We boarded after a time and T led us to first class. I've never ridden first class before, so it was a treat! The flight attendant brought us nuts and cookies, and then once the curtain was pulled separating us from the rest of the plane, she brought us drinks. I ordered Hennessey on the rocks. T had the same.

"T, I'm having so much fun!" I exclaimed as we soared about the clouds. "Nikki, have you ever heard of the mile high club?"

When the plane landed, there was another limo waiting for us. T had arranged for a series of appetizers to be waiting for us since it was past dinner. There was chicken wings and French fries, shrimp cocktail and vegetable dip. I am not going to lie; between the two of us, we ate every bite! Sex twice in as many hours makes one ravenous!

The limo took us to the Hilton Hotel of all places! Talk about opulence. The lobby alone was enough to make me want to never stay at another Holiday Inn.

T checked us in. "What about our bags?" I asked.

"They should be waiting for us in our suite."

"Suite?"

"Oops. I have big mouth. I had them shipped ahead." He took my arm and we strolled through the lobby; T looking right at home, me barely able to catch my breath because I was so excited!

"T! I can't believe this ... "

"I thought maybe we'd get cleaned up then go out to eat."

"Yeah, I can use a bath."

When we got to the room, again I was more impressed than before. Oh my God; fireplace, living room with wet bar, big screen TV and state of the art sound system. Double doors led to a bedroom in royal reds and golds. A king-sized bed, sitting high up and canopied, was the focal point. The room was breath taking! Our luggage set on luggage holders, champagne, chocolates and roses set on the bedside table. The bathroom made even T whistle. Double vanities, marble, round Jacuzzi already filled with bubbles. I sat on the side of the tub and placed my hand in the water. Damn...It was hot.

We stripped down and luxuriated in the tub together. I was a little tired but there was no way that I was going to let a little fatigue cause me to miss out on the New York nightlife!

We dressed and headed out. It was just after 9:00, but New York never sleeps! Since we weren't really hungry, we had dinner at a small pizzeria; the best pizza ever! We bought some subway passes and rode up to Greenwich Village where walked around hand in hand taking in the sights and sounds.

"I've never had more fun T. Ever. I love this city."

"I do too. I come here once or twice a year to shop." He said.

"Really?"

"Yeah. I've always wanted to come with someone."

"I can't believe it'd be difficult to find someone willing to go shopping with you in New York." He smiled.

"No ... just someone special." He kissed me lightly.

We headed back to the Hotel and decided to put the champagne in the fridge for tomorrow. The next day I got us up extra early. We had an excellent continental breakfast then I put on my walking shoes and prepared to do some serious shopping.

We hit Harlem first. I must have stopped in fifty stores! T whipped out his platinum card and wouldn't let me purchase so much as a tube of Mac lipstick using my own money!

When I started thinking that I had hit my limit, he began pointing out things I should buy. The only time he got the slightest bit annoyed with me is when I kept asking him if he was spending too much on me.

"Nikki, I'll tell you when you hit your limit. I do have a limit in mind, and you haven't hit it yet."

Okay … At the hair store, a tear actually ran down my cheek. I bought eight falls that I have yet to see back home! T was so loaded down with packages that we took a taxi back to the hotel.

After depositing our packages, we stopped at a coffee house in lieu of lunch and I saw Tony drink coffee for the first time. He got latte and I had a caramel frappucino.

"Come on," he said, taking my hand and leading me to another waiting limo.

"How do you do that?!" I screeched. How did he arrange all of this?! He just smiled. He then took me to some of the most expensive stores in New York.

"Are you crazy?" I whispered seriously when I looked at some of the price tags. Hey, I was content shopping in Harlem. He just smiled.

We went to the men's department and entered a private dressing room. T shopped from a catalogue and a salesman brought out his choices for him to try on. T was a fool for Armani, like I was a fool for fake hair. He found himself two suits that looked so expensive I wouldn't even peek at the price tag. But damn, did he look good. I refused to buy anything after checking out what he was buying for himself. The only way he got me to agree to allow him to buy something more for myself was by telling me he had tickets to an exclusive dance club and he started dropping names of stars and R&B and rap singers that showed up there regularly.

I bought a tan suede pants suit and matching cap. T insisted on me buying two pairs of shoes to match the outfit; one, a pair of matching suede ankle boots. The second; copper sling backs.

The limo took us back to the hotel once again, and once again, a bath was waiting for us. We were getting frisky in the tub when the doorbell rang. T put on a robe.

"That should be the masseuse. Dry off." I got out of the tub no longer surprised at anything T planned. How can anyone ever top a weekend like this?! A table was set up for each of us and we received a complete massage. It was nice, but it had nothing on what T could do!

Later, a stylist came up to do his hair and my make-up. Since I would be wearing one of my new wigs, she didn't need to do my hair.

I couldn't hang anymore; I took T into another room and insisted he listen to me. "T I'm not comfortable with all you're spending! You don't have to do all this-"

"Nikki, I would love to take credit for all of this, but it's a trade out package." A trade out is when we give our clients something they want and they give us something in return. "I negotiated this package as part of my bonus right in time for Sweetest Day. So all of this is free; the limos, hotel, romantic dinner for two and massage and stylist." He gave me a crooked smile. "You ruined it, you know. I could have taken all of the credit."

I squirmed, embarrassed. He gave me a suddenly serious look.

"Not many women would have a problem with spending my money." He said plainly.

I gave him a sincere look. "Those women aren't planning on keeping you forever." He kissed me.

Later, during our romantic dinner, I got up and dug in my bag for T's sweetest day present. I was so happy that I had spent the extra money on him.

"Happy Sweetest Day, T-baby." I sat on his lap kissing him.

"What? You didn't! When did you have time to do this?"

"Back home." He carefully unwrapped the gift, eyes widening when he caught sight of the watch.

"Nikki ... " he looked at me, impressed. "This is some serious bling." He lifted the watch and looked at the underside. "Platinum! Nikki, you shouldn't have!" I laughed and hugged him.

"Look who's talking!"

Later at the club we lived on the dance floor. I saw pro sports players, rappers—most of whom Tony had to tell me who they were. We even got our picture taken in front of one of those fake back-drops that are supposed to look like you're standing in a nuclear sunset, or on some pre-historic beach.

On our last night at the hotel, T made love to me slowly, making it last hours. I knew that I would no longer prefer the swift, spastic sex of the first few weeks. We had passed a milestone.

We'd gone to New York with a bag each and returned home looking like we'd been traveling around the world!

Remember when I said that you don't tell your girls too much about your man? Well, when I got home I TOLD!!

TONY

After the weekend in New York I was more convinced than ever before that I wanted to be with Nikki forever. But I felt like a man and woman should date at least 6 months before leaping into such an important decision. Still, I contemplated asking her if she wanted to live together.

I prayed that dinner at the parent's house would go well. I knew it would hurt Nikki's feelings if she didn't find a common ground with my mom. But, regardless, I'd made up my mind that I would not allow their relationship with each other affect me; affect us.

Sunday Nikki was cool and collected as we drove to my folk's house. She got her period and plus was drained from the hectic weekend. I knew all she really wanted to do was snuggle in bed.

"I hope your mom's not cooking anything ... different. My stomach's queasy." Silently, I hoped she didn't want to be funny and serve squid in ink sauce. Even I was squeamish about that.

When we got to Bond hill I pointed out points of past interest, like where me and my buddies played basketball, the park where we used to get drunk and high, and she remembered the house her favorite cousin and my old friend used to live. I pulled up into the driveway of my parent's brick two-bedroom house. It was small but one of the nicer houses on the street.

"Mom! We're here!" I entered without knocking.

"Toi?"

"Yes, Mom. I am an only child, remember?"

"Nikki? You here?"

"Yes, Mrs Yakamoto." She poked her head out of the kitchen as we entered the living room. She flipped her hand for us to stay out of the kitchen.

"Sit. I bring tea."

My dad ambled in from the family room where I'm sure he had been watching football.

"Hi Nikki. Nice to see you again."

"Hi Mr Yakamoto. How are you today?"

He smiled at her. "Good, wishing for retirement."

Mom brought out tea and sat it in front of us. "You too young to retire."

"Tell it to my old bones," he replied.

"What's for dinner?" I asked, not recognizing the smell.

"Pot roast." Dad and I stared at her.

She just returned the look. "What? You not like pot roast? You always cry for American food, now you not want pot roast." She winked at Nikki. "You like pot roast don't you, with potatoes and carrots?"

"I love pot roast, Mrs Yamamoto." Nikki smiled. Now what is my mom up to?

Dinner went wonderful. Mom asked Nikki a lot of questions about herself; what she liked to do. And Nikki asked Mom questions about living in Japan and

Japanese culture. The food was the best. There's not anything like going to your parents for a good home cooked meal.

After dinner Nikki insisted on helping Mom with the dishes so I was comfortable with following Dad to the family room to watch the rest of the game. I knew that if Mom would just make the effort she'd like Nikki, and vice versa.

NIKKI

Mrs Y surprised me with how friendly she was. I knew Tony did not pick up on this, but I noticed her staring at me when she thought I wasn't looking. I even thought I caught her smiling to herself.

Lord forgive me, but I wondered if she hadn't poisoned the food or something. Of course, that was crazy since we were all eating the same thing, including her.

After dinner she wanted me to join Mr Yakamoto and Tony in the family room. But I felt that if I was ever going to get to the bottom of the mystery of her sudden change in attitude, then I needed to be alone with her.

I could say a lot about Tony's mom, but one thing I couldn't say is that she's stupid. No sooner did the men leave the room did she turn to me and give me a hard look. It wasn't rude, but it wasn't nice either. If I were in a ring I would have put my "dukes" up.

"I see in your eyes how much you care for my son. I look in his eyes and I know he's in love."

Strangely, Mrs Yakamoto was no longer speaking in pigeon English.

"I love your son in a way that I've never loved any other man."

"My husband is right. Toi has never brought a girl home before, but I know he has had many girlfriends." She poured us each a glass of fruit juice.

"I hoped that I could influence Toi to marry an Asian. I've always wanted a large family but there were complications with Toi and I lost my uterus. Recently I began to worry that he wouldn't settle down, period. And more than anything ... " Mrs Yakamoto's eyes glistened as she looked away from me. "I want grandbabies. I want a daughter-in-law. I want holidays with a lot of laughter ... like when I was a girl in Japan." I looked down, heart aching in my chest at her honesty.

"Mrs Yakamoto, I love Tony ... but we've only been together a month. I don't know if ... six months down the line we may feel differently."

"Nikki I don't want you two to ever split up."

"Huh?" I asked stupidly.

"You're pregnant."

What the ... ?! "Mrs Yakamoto, I can assure you that I am not pregnant-"

She waved my words away. "It's too soon for you to know. But I see."

I crossed my arms self-consciously. "I'm ... a big woman but-"

"No, no, no." She made a motion with her spread fingers encircling her face. "It's here-"

"Mrs Yakamoto I just got my period, I can't be pregnant. I'm taking the pill." She shrugged and put aluminum foil over the remains of the roast.

"I'm never wrong Nikki. You are pregnant with my grandchild." She turned back to me smiling. "And I want to be a major part of his or her life."

I shook my head. "If I was pregnant, of course you'd be important in … our child's life." It was seriously creeping me out to even be talking like this. She smiled.

"You don't understand."

"Okay," I said warily.

"I want to baby sit her, I want to teach her how to cook Japanese meals, and to do the tea ceremony, I want to put ribbons in her hair, and if he's a boy I want to teach him to write Kanji. I want to take him to the market and brag on his first teeth, just the way my friends do. Nikki," she sighed. "I want a grand baby and I want a daughter-in-law."

"Even a black one?" I asked a bit peevishly. She didn't answer right away.

"I see in my head what a family looks like in Japan. But this is not Japan. And my eyes have to see what's in front of me." I smiled slowly and then nodded.

"I understand. I don't think I'm pregnant … but if I were … " I stopped, thinking of exactly how I wanted to phrase my next statement. "A baby would be both Japanese and African American. Both cultures are important." She smiled looking down at her hands.

"You're talking about Toi right now. I bet an African American mother who saw her African American son trying to be a white person would feel the way that I do and do the same things I have done." I knew she was right. "But it wasn't fair to him. Through you I can make it up to him."

"That'd be good."

She nodded. "Now we have good talk. You go to family room with Toi. Watch TV." Back was the pigeon English. It had been a good talk. I started out the kitchen then turned back to her.

"Do you think we can talk like this again?" She winked at me. "Any time you want." I decided that this conversation was just going to be between us. I went to the family room beaming.

Part III

The world is filled, with pimps and hoes
We'll just talk about those I knows
The world is mine, can't you see
I'm just trying to be all I can be
-Biggie Smalls

NIKKI

I was scratching my head, staring at the document in my hand and sighing for about the thirtieth time inside of ten minutes. I'd interviewed Dr Isadore Durdak. She was a seventy-two year old woman. During our interview I got the pleasure of learning all about her life. She was the first black female surgeon at Good Saints Hospital. She delivered the first set of living triplets at the hospital and she was the founder of the League of Black Medical Professionals; LBMP.

Obviously I wanted to grant her a loan. She would not have submitted the request for a refinance of her home if she had not needed it. But I just couldn't see myself doing it; especially after looking at this appraisal sheet.

I picked up the phone with another sigh and pressed an all-too familiar button.

"What's up, sweetness?" Oh, I wish Tony wouldn't do that! What if I'd had him on speakerphone? People were already giving us odd looks. The cat was pretty much out of the bag without him taking away all doubt.

"T, I need you to look over the Durdak approval. This one stinks to high heaven." I heard him grumble.

"I'll be right there."

He was rapping on my door less than sixty seconds later. He came inside, closing the door behind. "What's up, babe?"

I handed him the folder and he sat in the chair on the other side of my desk, examining the document. "And?" He shrugged.

"T, this lady has received three re-fi's in five years-"

He snorted. "So she's bad at money management-"

"Look at the value of the property!" I said excitedly. I saw him take a long soothing breath as if he was annoyed. He continued to study the document, finally peeking at me over the top of his wire rimmed glasses.

"Do you see how the value of the house keeps going up? At the first re-fi it was two hundred forty-five thousand. Now, five years later it's three hundred thousand ... but none of the other properties in the area have gone up in value like that. This is predatory, T!"

He frowned. "Shhh." He was right, I was getting overly excited and I calmed down. "Nikki, you aren't a real estate agent any longer so why are you even looking at any of this? The company hired reputable appraisers that know their jobs." He slid the paper back across the desk towards me, looking cool and controlled as if he was talking to one of the companies tax attorneys. My mouth was hanging open in complete surprise. I had expected him to share my outrage, and here he was acting like I was out of line!

I snapped my mouth shut and gave him a calm look to match his as I smoothed my palms over the document. "Ok. Well I'm not going to approve this."

Tony took off his glasses and placed them in the breast pocket of his very expensive suit. "Nikki, why are you tripping?"

"I don't think I am." I put the document back in the folder. "If anyone is 'tripping' then it's you."

He frowned again. "I'm going to have to pay for this when we get home, aren't I?"

"You're the one who can't separate work from home or you wouldn't be calling me 'sweetie', and 'babe' here at the office ... so don't expect me to do so." I gave him a chilly look.

He paused. "Fair enough." He came to his feet slowly and despite the fact that I was so pissed that I was livid, I still felt a spark at how incredibly sexy he was.

He held out his hand. "The file." I wanted to throw it at him but that would have been childish. "Why are you making this so brand new? Nikki, the job description hasn't changed."

I cocked my head to the side in disbelief and jumped to my feet. "You know what? I turn a blind eye when it's some young vacant-headed trust fund baby. But not an old lady that has moved to the top of her field and now can't afford to live!" His eyes rose to the ceiling and I could have sworn he was counting to three. "Toi Yakamoto, I know you aren't standing there like you are aggravated at me!"

His dark, almond shaped eyes, moved from where he was watching the ceiling to meet mine. His face was turning dark. How did he have the right to be mad because I was speaking the truth?

"Nikkita DaNeen Mason, don't get it twisted. Mrs Durdak has over fifty thousand dollars worth of credit card bills — and they are not to the local grocery store so that she can buy food to eat! That lady owes Macy's, Speigels, Saks, Parisians and about ten others! She's acquired this debt in the short time since her last re-fi. When you turn down this loan, how is she supposed to pay those bills?! Don't think that old lady is not every bit as sharp as she was thirty years ago! She knows the deal. She'll re-fi and will not outlive this mortgage. Then her Estate will pay it off. Who does that hurt, Nikki? It's what she wants!"

I narrowed my eyes at him; hurt that he didn't see that just because a person needed a loan didn't mean that we needed to exploit them and their hardship. "And what if she doesn't understand that her house isn't really valued at three hundred thousand dollars? It's probably not even valued at two fifty! What if she doesn't know that she will be paying damn near a hundred thousand more than the value of the thing?! You do not see that as wrong, T?!"

He shook his head and tapped the folder against his palm. "Whatever." Then he turned to leave.

Whatever?! Without thinking I picked up my ink pen and hurled it at him. It bounded off the back of his head and he froze, back stiff.

Oh my God ... what the fuck? What was I doing?! I had never thrown anything at anybody in my life. It was just that his controlled manner was pissing me off.

He turned and gave me incredulous look. "Ok ... that's it!" He locked the door and stormed back to me. I wanted to cringe but instead I squared my shoulders. He slammed the folder back on my desk and pointed his finger at me.

"You've been working here for almost a year and every step of the way it's a battle!"

"Don't you point your finger at me!" He was pointing his finger at me! My face was hot. Who was he to put his finger in my face?!

He lowered his hand and placed both on his narrow hips. His suit jacket was unbuttoned and his crisp blue shirt was cut just perfectly for his compact, muscular form. His tie was almost the exact blue as the shirt and looked awesome on him. "You know what you sound like?" His voice was back to being controlled again. "You sound like one of those cigarette industry ads where they tell you why you shouldn't smoke even though everybody already knows why you shouldn't! I'm just saying; you're kinda crazy to be working for the cigarette industry, Nikki!"

I pointed my finger at him. "No I'm not! I didn't know that cigarettes were bad for you-I mean, I didn't know this place was so crooked!"

"What?"

"You know what I'm saying."

"No I don't."

I threw my hands up in the air. "You're just being an asshole."

His already slanted eyes narrowed even more. "That's it!" Before I knew it he had rounded the desk and was up in my face. He kept moving forward until I was backed up against the wall. It didn't matter that he was shorter than me, weighed less than me, when his body moved mine backwards, I was going nowhere but backwards!

When there was nowhere else that I could go, Tony's lips pushed against mine. I turned my head defiantly even though my heart was pounding in my chest, and a pulse had just begun to beat between my thighs. When my lips weren't available to him, he just kissed my neck, his mouth moving over my skin roughly. I felt his hands grip the material of my skirt and hike it up high, over my thighs.

Despite my resolve to be outraged and angry, I groaned and pushed my lower body against his. I felt the breath catch in his throat. Roughly I put my hands in his hair and gripped it in my fist. He released my skirt and gripped my ass, pulling me against him just as he was pushing his pelvis roughly against my own. Mmmm, I felt him rock hard. Then he must have been working up to this state while we argued …

He was squeezing great handfuls of my ass and grinding against me. Tony loved a big ass; in his hands, slapping against his face, didn't matter to him! He began pushing my panties and nylons down.

"Don't rip them." I said breathlessly.

He dug his fingers into the delicate material until they poked through, shredding them! Then he continued pushing down my panties roughly, almost ripping them, too, while his lips sucked and kissed my neck. I was still pulling his dark, coiffed hair and he didn't seem to notice. Suddenly he was yanking me back to my chair, collapsing into it and pulling me over his lap!

"What the fuck-?"

Then I felt his palm come down sharply onto my naked ass cheek.

POW

He did it again as I lay across his lap, skirt hiked up over my bottom, panties and ripped nylons pulled down enough to expose my ass to his palm.

POW

Repeatedly he spanked my ass, and none too lightly! I kept trying to push off of his lap, but just like he had backed me against the wall, he kept me prone across his lap.

"Are you crazy? Let me up!" I tried to keep my voice hushed but I was surprised ... and though I hate to admit it, becoming even more aroused, despite the fact that my ass stung.

POW!

"Ow!" I reached behind me to rub my stinging ass but he gripped my hand.

"Move that hand or you're going to get more!"

"This is ridiculous-"

POW! POW!

I moved my hand. I couldn't believe that he was spanking me as if I was a little kid. I suddenly felt his palm moving gently over my skin. I peeked at him. He met my eyes and his lips rose into a slight smile.

"Asshole ... "

"Don't tempt me." He said while stroking the crack of my ass with his thumb.

I squirmed and moaned. "Oh ...

"Bend over your desk, love."

"T ... " I felt him leap to his feet, almost sending me tumbling to the floor. But his strong arms hefted me up to my feet and the next second I was lying face down across it. I felt him fumbling at his pants and my breath came in shallow, excited puffs. He plunged into my wet opening, mercilessly.

I can't help that I love it hard and fast and I started groaning loudly! T quickly clamped his hand across my mouth but he didn't stop pumping in and out of me. I gripped the desk and hung on as he worked me roughly from behind.

This was turning me on more than I could have ever imagined! Maybe it was the fighting to stay quiet, or maybe it was my mostly passive boyfriend going wild, but all I knew is that I was on the verge of exploding. If his hand wasn't pressed to my mouth I would have been screaming for him to fuck me harder!

He folded his body over mine and I heard him whisper harshly between gritted teeth. "I'm going to pull out. If you want to cum you better do it soon!"

Then he smacked my ass again and resumed his pounding.

I didn't need to wait! I pushed back against him and we crashed together. With a loud whimper I exploded! Tony smacked my ass again knowing how much I loved it and I trembled, my entire body shaking. His hand over my mouth kept in my wild, passionate cries.

"Nikki!" He whimpered before quickly pulling out of me. He couldn't remove his hand from me because I still hadn't quieted, but his other hand evidently worked his erection because before I knew it, I felt warm spurts over my ass. I sucked in as much breath as I could from between Tony's fingers and he finally uncovered my mouth.

My body was clenching at nothing as I fell from my orgasm. My pelvis continued to roll and I felt Tony stroke my recently waxed pussy, teasing my clit until my body jerked in a mini climax, and I finally collapsed, sated.

I closed my eyes tiredly and felt Tony move about, reaching for tissue to clean my backside of his cum. He moved again and I heard my desk drawer open where he retrieved air freshener and liberally sprayed the room to rid it of the obvious smell of sex. Next he picked up the fallen items from my messy desk, working around me while I lay there limply. Lastly he pulled up my panties, pulled down my torn nylons, smoothed down my skirt and pulled me up gently, sitting me in my chair.

I gave him a hooded look and he kneeled before me, removed my shoes and pulled off my stockings. Instead of throwing them into my trash he opened the drawer and shoved them into my bag.

"Those nylons cost nearly twenty dollars." I said accusingly.

His hands ran up my legs before replacing my shoes onto my feet. "Those pretty brown legs don't need nylons, love."

"T ... " I sighed.

"Come on, straighten your clothes." He had already righted his and looked as innocent as a babe. No one would know that only five minutes before he had been pounding my pussy and spanking my ass!

He meticulously straightened my desk once again as I stood on shaky legs and smoothed my suit. I was fixing my make-up when he picked up the Durdak folder and headed to the door.

"So what are you going to do with that?"

He didn't pause or turn around. "Deny it. Just like you said."

What I was unsure of, was if he had intended to do that all along?

TONY

It was Friday and I was on my way to play basketball with the guys. On the drive over, I decided to go past Mrs Durdak's house. She lived in Silverton. It was a mixed community but over the years had gone through a slight decline. The recession hadn't made matters any better.

Nikki had made me think about things that I had long ago stopped caring about. In my pursuit to become a Department Manager I had started looking at my customers as products instead of people. Would I sell my mother a house that was valued at only two thirds of the sale price? Would I kick somebody's ass for doing that to my mother?!

It was dusk when I turned down the elderly lady's street. I didn't need full light to see that the house was in no way close to being in good condition. It was big. That was all that I could say about it. There was a time when it probably was nice, but that was probably ten years ago.

The house was in terrible need of a paint job. The gutters were falling apart. The porch railing needed repairs, some of the shutters were dangling...yet the yard was nice. There were beautiful flowers, and even a fountain, though it wasn't currently working.

I didn't need to see the inside to know that there was no way this house was valued at three hundred

grand; even if it had solid gold walls inside! I drove
on to the Rec Center where Jay had a membership,
thinking about Nikki and our earlier argument.

Nikki was still a little pissed at me even though
she wouldn't admit it. She chewed my ass for fucking
her in the office. And she was right. That is not
something we do often. As a matter of fact, we work
ourselves up to being hot and bothered and wait until
we get home before doing anything, which makes for
crazy sex!

But I had just been so worked up, and that pent
up energy had to go somewhere. Nikki and I have
been together almost four months. I'm, without a
doubt, in love with her. I love everything about
Nikkita Mason, from her hair weaves, to her full,
voluptuous body and big booty. I love her smile and
the twinkle in her eyes and the way she gets horny if I
just lick my lips. She is everything I want.

But damn if she isn't the moodiest woman I've
ever known; and bossy, and a know-it-all. But I
wouldn't have her any other way … I wouldn't know
what to do with a docile woman. I guess I just have to
be happy that I'm the one that has her, and not my old
friend Dean.

I winced at the thought of seeing Dean today. It
had taken him a few weeks to dare show his face
again after the stunt he pulled at Nikki's. He'd come
over drunk, calling her out of her name and pissed
that I was over there. I got in his ass and he'd been
keeping a low profile. I hadn't mentioned the incident

to Jay, who is Nikki's cousin, and Dean eventually ended up slithering back into the group.

Back in High School, the five of us were inseparable. Back then I was called T-Baby, then there was Jay-Dog, Dean; also known as Big Daddy D, Budda; who was a light skinned black dude, pale like butter, and Pac; because he could rap. Now we were men in our thirties who broke away from family and work when we could to shoot hoops, listen to Jay D.J. or watch a game at someone's house.

The guys were already waiting for me on the court. "You're usually the first one here." Pac said as he high fived me.

"I had to make a quick stop." They all razzed me since they assumed the 'quick stop' was Nikki. I was the butt of the joke almost every time we got together, but it was all in good fun. Dean wisely kept all comments to himself. And no one but me knew that he had dated Nikki for a few weeks.

We played hard for a while, and then the guys began getting distracted by the girls in the bleachers cat-calling us. I had successfully ignored them before realizing that all of my boys had come out of their shirts; including Budda, who still looked like Heavy D.

"Take off your shirt!" Someone yelled at me. They were a bunch of giggling girls. I waved at them dismissively.

"Why you playing hard?!" Dean said with a grin. "Those girls are looking for some Jackie Chan action."

We had taken a breather and I wiped my face on my t-shirt, exposing my stomach momentarily and someone whistled amidst more girly giggling.

"Because those girls are young enough that I'd want to see some ID from them."

"Ah come on, I'm a married man." Pac said before taking a long drink from his water bottle. He eyed the girls. "But nothing wrong with putting on a show."

"Come on!" A really bold girl stood up in the bleachers, obviously egged on by her friends. "Let's see what you got under that shirt!"

I shook my head and Budda nudged me.

"Show us what you got under your shirt!" He yelled back.

Even Jay had to tell him to chill. Dean walked over to the bleachers flexing his considerable muscles and the girls whooped loudly. Everyone was watching him, which I'm sure he loved.

I poured water over my head to cool off and then pulled off my shirt and wiped away the wetness with it. I tossed it over to the sidelines, out of the way.

"Damn ... " I heard someone say.

"Thank you!"

"Yeah, thanks Mister. You look good!"

"Can I have your number?"

I just bowed. "Now can we finish playing, Dean?" He smirked and we resumed our game.

After the game, when I went back to retrieve my shirt, it was gone.

NIKKI

While Tony went out with his boys, I decided to hang with my girls. I've been guilty of blowing them off recently. It's hard to choose a girl's night out over a professional massage by your sexy boyfriend.

We met at TGIF Fridays for dinner and then we were going to catch a Tyler Perry movie.

"Is that a Louis Vuitton bag? A real one?"

I smiled. "Of course it's the real thing." As if I'd admit it if it was just a knock-off.

"Is that one of the things your boyfriend bought you on your New York shopping spree?"

I loved my friends because none of them acted low-class and catty. They checked out the bag, admiring it with no drama. They wanted a run down on everything I bought on the trip. It would have been low-class of me to tell them how much he'd spent on me, so I didn't.

We finally got seated in the crowded restaurant; whose idea was it to go to a FRIDAYS on a Friday? I stared at the menu not sure what I wanted. Nothing listed really interested me. I was hungry, but not for anything heavy.

Everyone had given their orders and I was still undecided. I passed my menu back to the waitress. "Can I just have a bowl of fettuccini noodles but plain; no sauce. Then I want a side of ranch dressing, but microwave it so that it's warm. Then I want a side of fried green beans but with cold ranch. Got it? Oh, and a glass of lemonade."

The table was absolutely quiet and all of my friends were staring at me.

"What?"

Belinda was the one to speak first. "Girl ... are you pregnant?"

"What?" I gave her a perplexed look.

"Um ... yuck."

I laughed. "Stop trying to make a story where there is none!"

Shaunda eyed me suspiciously. "You got that glow; either you're pregnant or oily."

"She does!" Belinda almost screamed.

My stomach began to drop as I touched my face. "I'm not pregnant. I haven't missed my period, I'm on the pill-" I was listing these facts more for myself than them.

"None of that matters. I heard about a girl that had a cycle every month for the first six months of her pregnancy. And the pill is only 99.9 percent-"

I threw my napkin at her and it hit her square in the face.

"Moodiness!" Shaunda piped in. "That's another symptom."

I thought fleetingly of Tony's mother. Three months ago, she had told me that I was pregnant ... I had dismissed it because I'd been having my cycle. She hadn't brought it up again even as our relationship continued to grow. This is ridiculous! How could I even be considering this as a possibility?

Taking in my expression they stopped joking at my expense. "Go get yourself a pregnancy test." Belinda said seriously.

I took a drink of lemonade and changed the subject.

TONY

After hanging with the guys, I went back to my place to shower. I knew Nikki would be out with two of her girlfriends for a while. They were planning dinner and a movie and they would probably spend a lot of time getting caught up. I took Wu-Tang for a walk. I loved how Nikki didn't mind when I brought my dog over to her place. Some women would have made me keep her outside, or made all kinds of rules. The only rule that she had was no dog on the furniture or in the bed, and definitely no doggy kisses.

It was about ten when Wu-Tang and I got to her place. I was surprised that her car was parked out front. She must have changed her mind, but she should have called me and I would have come over earlier ... unless she was still pissed. I sighed. I let myself in with my key and saw that the front room was dark. She must be in bed already.

"Stay out here, girl." I went into the bedroom and shut the door so that the dog wouldn't follow. But Nikki wasn't in bed. She was just standing there watching me.

"Didn't you go?" I asked, giving her a peck on the cheek.

She nodded. "Yeah I didn't feel like a movie so I came home early."

"You okay?" I rubbed her arms. She looked tense.

"Y-yeah." She nodded. "Um … I'm pregnant."

"Um … what did you say?" I'm almost positive that I heard her wrong. What are all of the words that rhyme with pregnant … ? I was silently straining for some ideas.

She smiled sheepishly and whispered, "I'm pregnant."

I rubbed her arms again and I'm sure that I had a stupid look on my face. "Seriously?"

"I wouldn't joke about this-"

"Wow … a baby." I started chuckling, even though my heart was slamming in my chest. I pulled her into my arms and kissed her.

She gave me an amazed look. "You're happy? We've only been together four months and … "

I kissed her again. "I don't care. I love you."

She smiled. "I love you, too."

I frowned. "How?" She's on the pill and has been since we got together.

She shrugged. "I have no idea. I mean, I've not missed my cycle."

"You're sure that you are?"

She pulled out of my arms and hurried to the connecting bathroom and brought back one of those pregnancy test sticks. I took it but it didn't take a rocket scientist to see that the great big pink plus sign meant positive. She went back to the bathroom for the box and I spent fifteen minutes reading about false negatives ... which did take a rocket scientist to understand.

"I'll make an appointment with my doctor Monday."

I grimaced. "Monday? Well it's Friday. We have to wait until Monday?"

She shrugged. "We could go to the free clinic tomorrow, if their open on Saturdays."

I nodded. "Let's do that."

It was hard to sleep that night. I kept thinking about how hard I'd fucked her today ... Shit, I'd spanked her, too! And I couldn't stop thinking about all of the rough sex we've had. Then I couldn't reconcile the fact that she's on birth control and has had a regular cycle. I mean ... what the fuck?! But then there was the idea of a little baby growing in my woman's body and that I'd placed it there. I was going to be a father. A little Asian, African-American kid would be looking up to me for guidance. The idea was frightening and awesome all at once.

The next morning, neither of us lingered in bed the way we usually do on Saturdays. We hurried to the free clinic, and as usual, was the center of attention. I held her hand nervously trying not to think about the reason that the other people were here.

The free clinic might be free but it is not fast! We finally got called back, they asked us a lot of questions, and then she finally got to pee in a cup. We went back into the waiting area to wait again.

We had skipped breakfast and Nikki was on her third bag of chips when they finally called us back.

The woman, nurse, doctor, whatever she was, looked at us from atop her bifocals. She smiled. "Congratulations. You are pregnant." Nikki and I smiled at each other.

"How many months am I?" She asked.

"We can usually get a pretty good guess based on your last menstrual cycle but based on the information you've told me you will need to make an appointment for an ultrasound. We don't do that here so you will need to set up an appointment with your regular physician. Now if you don't have one, we can refer you to-"

"No, no. We have a doctor."

She smiled at us again. "Any questions?" We probably had tons but we were both excited to get out of there. She gave us several brochures and we hurried out. Nikki just kept grinning.

"Where do you want to go for breakfast? Mommy's choice." I was grinning myself. I'm going to be a DADDY!

"I want to go to your Mom and Dad's house."

My smile disappeared. Oh shit ... my mother!

NIKKI

We got to Tony's parent's house. We hadn't called first. Mrs Y liked our impromptu visits even if she always wore a sour expression. I liked her and I knew for a fact that she liked me. Maybe it hadn't begun that way, but we were stuck with each other; for better or for worse.

Tony walked in the door as he always did, without knocking or saying hi. "Mom? Dad? Nikki and I are here." They were in the kitchen having lunch and I was happy as hell! God, I was starving! We all exchanged hugs and kisses; something I'd introduced to them. I'm a hugger, can't help it and T's family was very reserved. But I know that they are very happy that I have pushed them into the realm of affection. I've even seen them touching each other a few times.

"What brings you two out to our part of the world?" Mr Y asked. He was great. He always made things easy. He was finishing up a sandwich. Grrr ... why couldn't it have been fish fritters?! I would give my right arm for a fish fritter!

T had a mischievous look in his eyes when he spoke. "We were at the free clinic and that's not so far from here so we figured that we'd stop by and see what you two were having for lunch-"

"Free clinic? Why you two go to free clinic? That for people with no money! You two got money!" Mrs Y said, taking the bait.

"Yeah, Nikki needed to get tested." I smacked his arm. "Kidding, gosh. We took a pregnancy test." T got up and moved to the refrigerator. "What's for lunch?" His mother smacked him in the back of the head.

"Toi! If you know what good for you, you won't make me mad!" She said in broken English.

He chuckled. "Okay okay. We're pregnant."

Mrs Y screamed. I mean, she literally bellowed. I think Mr Y almost had a heart attack because she was so thrilled by the news ... or possibly by the bellowing, I'm not sure. I was hugged and kissed by the both of them. Mrs Y gave me a clandestine wink and I hid my smile.

"You men make us a real lunch." Mrs Y said while sitting down. "Nikki is going to be a mother and I'm going to be a grandmother!" She clapped her hands sharply. "Come on, get to it!"

Tony bowed good-naturedly. "Yes your majesties. Any requests?"

"Fish fritters." I said quickly.

Mrs Y gave me a quick look. "Oh no. No fish fritters for you! Mercury in the fish; bad for baby." My mouth dropped. No fish fritters?

"Don't Japanese women eat sushi?" I probed.

"Sushi fish is best grade fish! You eat sushi, then fine."

"We can make the fish fritters from sushi grade fish ... " I tried.

Mrs Y scowled. "Fish fritters? I teach you correct cooking technique for fritters so you can cook correct for my grandbaby. No sushi meat in fish fritters!" I poked out my lip and T smiled at me as if to say, and you thought she drove me crazy for no reason. In the end we had a quick stir-fry with leftovers from the fridge. I ate so much that I was practically bursting at the seams. So in the end I guess we were all happy.

Tony

My secretary, Debbie rang my phone while I was sitting in my office contemplating the appointment that we had later today. It had taken a week for us to get the ultrasound appointment and though I wanted the earliest possible one of the day, Nikki made me see reason in that the both of us taking off work would be pretty suspicious. So we made an evening appointment.

I was thinking about the appointment when the phone rang. I pressed the receive button. "Yes, Debbie?"

"Mr Milton is on the other line."

"Put him through." I kept it on speaker. Roger Milton was my manager and he answered only to the owner of the company. He and I were on very good working terms. He had helped me to get the Department Manager's job in the first place.

"Hey Roger. How's it going?"

"Tony," he sighed. "I'm looking at some figures that have me concerned." I came to attention. Getting a call from my boss was routine, getting a call from him stating that he was concerned was quite another matter.

"Okay. What seems to be the problem?"

"The Durdak account." Shit.

"Ahh." I said.

"Underwriting had already approved it and then it was denied by Nikkita." I picked up the phone, taking it off speaker.

"There were some ... extenuating circumstances that had come to light. It raised some concerns with her, and after I reviewed the file I had to agree." I waited quietly for the hammer to drop.

"Come to my office."

Wham!

"On my way."

P

"Babe, you seem really quiet." Nikki said, rubbing my hand as we drove to the appointment. "Are you anxious about the ultrasound?"

I hadn't wanted to talk about work related things when we were on our way to something so important. I smiled. "No, I'm excited about that. We get to see the first pictures of our baby. Do we want to know the sex?"

"No! Besides, I think it will be too soon for that."

"Hmmm, true. But we're going to need to start thinking of blackanasian names."

She laughed. "I think that will be easy."

"Not for a boy. Japanese male names are very anime; like Yoshi, Tanaka, Yuri. And those are just the common ones. Then there's Akihito and Kiyoshi ... and I just don't want my son to feel 'stuck' like I felt, with a jacked-up name that didn't match any of my friends." Toi Yakamoto was not an easy name to have as a child growing up in an all black neighborhood!

She rubbed my knuckles. "We won't do that to our child. But I want his or her name to represent both cultures."

I nodded, proud that I'd found a woman that cared about such things. "Well our baby will definitely be representing the Japanese culture with the last name Yakamoto."

"Mason." She said casually.

"Mason?" I almost ran off the road.

"Yeah." She gave me a smile. "My baby will have the same last name that I have."

My face relaxed. Ahhh, fishing for a proposal. Well it had been a week since she announced her pregnancy. But I had to do things with a special style. I mean, I only intend to propose to a woman once in my life and I want it to be memorable for the both of us. I was thinking about a trip somewhere romantic ...

Nikki poked me and when I looked at her again she was sticking her tongue out at me.

"Be careful where you point that thing. I might put it to good use." I pulled into a parking space and we went hand in hand to the radiology department where we were instructed to wait for our name to be called. There were a lot of pregnant women waiting, but very few men. I was being watched like I was some God. I intended to remember the looks and I intended to be here with Nikki throughout this process.

When our name was finally called I was feeling strange. I was getting into the idea of being a Dad, even though I hadn't thought much about it before Nikki. I figured it would be a natural progression once I found the right woman—but I had been focused only on finding her. And now that I had, I just hadn't thought further. Now it was all that I could think about--her, our baby, a family together. It was both wondrous and frightening.

Once inside the office, she climbed up on the examining table and the technician covered her belly with a towel, pulling down the waistband of her skirt and tucking the towel under so that it wouldn't get wet.

Nikki lifted her blouse exposing her belly and the technician grabbed a bottle of gel. "Okay, Mom. This may be a little cold." She liberally spritzed her belly and Nikki reached out and gripped my hand.

"Okay. So we are going to take measurements of baby to determine an age." The lady gestured to a monitor. "You can watch the monitor but it will be unlikely that you will be able to see clearly at this stage. Mom, your last period was on the eighteenth of the month?" Nikki nodded.

The lady pressed a wand to Nikki's belly and began rolling it, pressing fairly hard. Immediately we heard the whomp whomp whomp sound of a heartbeat.

"Baby's heartbeat is very strong." We were all glued to the monitor and plain as day, there he/she was! The technician was clicking away taking pictures and measurements and all I could think was that ... this is freaking really happening! There is my kid ...

Nikki looked at me and I didn't care that the technician was in the room clicking away. I bent down and kissed her lightly. "I love you." I mouthed. She mouthed it back.

"Alright." The technician finally said. "We will have some pictures for you to take home. She took the towel and wiped off the gel and was about to pull down her blouse when Nikki stopped her.

"No no. I need another towel. This is a pure silk blouse and I don't want a drop of gel on it!" The woman handed Nikki a fresh towel and she concentrated on finding every trace of gel, mumbling under her breath when she discovered traces of the potentially silk-ruining substance.

"Okay, Mom and Dad, you can go back to the office and I will work up the measurements." I kissed her neck as we sat in the small plastic chairs. Is it normal for me to feel horny right now? I had this feeling of, 'I am man! I have created life!' Now I wanted to plunge into her and spread more life giving fluid!

Only a few moments later the technician returned to the office and proudly handed us the first pictures of Baby Mason-Yakamoto.

"The baby has your big head, T." She said.

"Wow ... " I couldn't unglue my eyes from the sight of the teeny slope of the nose and the impression of eyes and little arms and legs. Damn ... my kid ...

"So you are sixteen weeks. That gives you a due date of November-"

"How many weeks?" Nikki interrupted, frowning.

"Sixteen." The technician repeated. After that it was hard for me to hear anything else. Nikki and I have only been together for about thirteen or fourteen weeks. This wasn't my baby. This was Dean's baby.

Nikki

I felt sick. Not the type that makes you feel like you need to run to the bathroom and vomit but the type of sick like you need to have someone pull the plug on life support because it can go nowhere but downhill.

"How accurate are those weeks?"

"Good question Mom. They are fairly accurate, give or take a week or two." Give or take a week or two! The difference between a week or two was the difference between my life crashing down around me or soaring forward! Tony and I have only been together three and a half months. That's not sixteen weeks!

I looked at the man that I loved with all of my heart and soul. He was absolutely motionless. His face was like a stone statue. His eyes were like two black chips of coal.

We left the office and I made an appointment for later that week to visit a prenatal doctor and then we went back to the car. Tony still hadn't said a word. I didn't know what I wanted him to say ... I mean, I do know what I wanted him to say, but he just drove us back to my apartment. On the way, I finally had to break the unbearable silence.

"Tony ... " He glanced at me. "She said it could be off by one or two weeks."

"But she didn't say off by two or three." And there it was. He had already accepted that this baby wasn't his. I felt like shit. When we got to the apartment I got out the car but Tony didn't. I turned and looked at him.

"I need to clear my head, Nikki. I'm going to go back to my place." I nodded. "Send Wu-Tang out, please." Again I nodded. Wu-Tang got to be with him, but I didn't. Right now I needed to be with him. But I know that he needed to be away from me.

Once Wu-Tang and Tony were gone I sank down on the couch and cried.

TONY

I dug the leash out of the glove compartment and then Wu-Tang and I went to the dog park. I put on my sunglasses and took off my suit jacket leaving it in the car. I wish I had stopped home to change into jeans or something but I wanted to walk the trails and think. My head felt crowded and I couldn't put my thoughts in order.

One minute my brain had been filled with images of me, Nikki, and our child. The next was Nikki fucking Dean. God help me, but the vision disgusted me. I couldn't stop seeing the three of us on the Maury Polvich show doing the big DNA reveal and Maury opening the manila folder and announcing; Toi Yakamoto—you are NOT the father ...

I sat down on a bench and Wu-Tang cocked her head at me as if to say, 'Iz gonna be ai'ight, Boss.'

"I might be, you know. There's a chance ... right?"

Wu-Tang gave me a baleful look. I sighed. This day is going from bad to worse; first Richard chews my ass and gives me my first reprimand as a Department Manager, and now this. Worse is that I didn't even want to face Nikki and I was going to be forced to give her an official reprimand as well.

I already knew that there was no way that she was going to take this lying down. She was going to be all in my face over this. Thing is, there was one side of me that resented the fact that she wouldn't just do the job, while there was the other side that was proud of her for having principals that she stood up for. Still, it was easy to have standards when your boyfriend was your buffer. But I had to make the same decision that I'm going to have to challenge Nikki to make; whether to let her standards pay her bills or her job.

My phone rang and I pulled my thoughts back to the present with an unpleasant jolt. I didn't want to talk to Nikki but I wasn't much more relieved to see that it wasn't Nikki calling but my Mom. Argh. I couldn't do this now. I returned the phone to my pocket unanswered. Sighing I came to my feet. "Come on. Let's go home, Wu."

Nikki

I never thought that I'd be that woman; the one that didn't know who the father of her unborn baby is. I didn't sleep a wink last night. Tony didn't come back to the apartment or call. The phone did ring several times but it was Mrs Y. Every time I heard it, I'd start bawling all over again. I'm not the crying type and I know that being pregnant floods you with lots of hormones—so it's not just that my heart is breaking.

I considered calling in sick but I was anxious to see Tony. He'd have to say something to me. He might disappear for a time after work hours, but not during work.

It was almost noon before I heard from him. My office phone rang and the red light indicator showed that the call was coming from his office. I picked up anxiously, not even aware of how tense I'd been all morning.

"Hello?"

"Nikki. Hey."

"Hey."

"How are you?" He asked quietly.

"I … I'm ok." I lied.

"Look, can you come to the office? I need to talk to you."

"Oh. Ok, sure." I was rather surprised that he'd want to have this talk at work. I hung up quickly and straightened my jacket. I had to keep it buttoned to hide the bulge of my tummy. Now that I knew that I was pregnant my extended tummy looked like a pregnant belly and not just a woman that had one too many burritos at lunch. On the up side, at least I wouldn't have to go on that crash diet that I had been planning.

I rapped on his door once and entered.

"Hey."

"Come on in. Close the door." He stood up and I noted the strained look on his face. He hadn't slept well himself, I guess.

I suddenly wrung my hands. "Tony, look. I'm so sorry. But I didn't intend for this to happen. You have to know that this is throwing me for a loop just as much as it is you-"

He held up his hand to stop me. "Nikki, I didn't ask you to come for that. I wanted to talk to you about something else."

"Something else?" I frowned. What else was there?

"Please, sit down." He gestured to the leather chair in front of his desk that he'd purchased from Ikea. It showed just how much he appreciated nice things that he would spend his own money to furnish the office in a way that was comfortable for him. Despite his connection with all things African-American, his office reflected his Asian heritage. He had two very large and very expensive bonsai trees.

He had a large silk screen wall covering of Koi fish and lilies in a pond. He had a beautiful tea set that I knew he actually used, especially when he had a rough day. He would drink tea from leaves that he actually hand mixed. Tony was a man that had so much diversity that being with him was like being on a journey—one that you would be a fool to turn down.

I sat down. "What did you want to talk to me about?"

"The Durdak account."

"What?" Of all of the things that I could imagine coming from his mouth—that wasn't one of them.

"Mrs Durdak filed a complaint for being denied the loan. There's a report made against the company with the Better Business Bureau because the loan officer had already told her that the deal would go through."

I was in complete shock. My mouth was hanging open. "Well the loan officer should have never done that!" This wasn't the first time that a client had to have the rug pulled out from under their feet because some idiot had jumped the gun!

He shrugged. "It's not against company rule to tell a client that their loan should have no trouble. It wasn't the loan officer that had done anything wrong, it was us."

"Us?!"

"Yes. We did. We make loans and we use homes as collateral. That's our job."

"Oh, not this again-"

He held up his hand once more. "Wait, let me finish. Please." I nodded, with a sigh. "Not to beat a dead horse. I understand your position. I've even shared it. The point is we have a directive. And based on that, we should have passed the account to be approved."

"But-"

"Nikki!" He said sharply. "I'm not done. Please. Let me finish." My brow gathered at his tone but I kept quiet. "I'm not going to argue with you. You and I as a couple can debate, but me as your supervisor ... there is no room for that. This is the job you have. If you don't do it, then it will be reflected on your evaluation."

My heart slammed against my ribcage. "My ... evaluation?" I could not believe that he was sitting there so calmly threatening my job. How did we get here? Oh yeah ... the fact that I might be having another man's baby is how we got here. Is that what this was about for him?

He put on glasses and opened a file that had my name on it. "Consider this your official counseling session. So after this, if you don't follow protocol then it will be reflective on your critical job elements which would then lower your evaluation." He retrieved a form and passed it to me. "Sign this stating that we have discussed your expectations."

I couldn't believe this, his attitude, his detachedness. I was more confused and hurt than angry. I slid the form to me and looked at it closely. Then I picked up the ink pen and signed and dated it.

I passed the form back to him without saying another word.

He nodded. "I don't have anything else." I walked out the door without another look at him and he watched me wordlessly. I went straight to the restroom and got very ill.

TONY

That could not have gone worse. All I had wanted to do is to avoid a long drawn out debate, but instead I came off looking like I was trying to punish her. Okay, and the truth of the matter is I had wanted to punish her. I don't know why, I mean, I'm sure she wanted to be in a position of not knowing whose baby she was carrying just as much as I did. Damn, I needed to apologize. I got up and hurried out of my office but Debbie stopped me before I had even gotten two steps.

"Tony, Richard wants you to take this to Mrs Durdak before five o'clock." She handed me an envelope and I opened it. It was her check. I grimaced. So I was to give her a personal apology. Fine. I hurried down the corridor to Nikki's office and was stopped again by one of my employees.

"Tony, can you sign off on this? I promised Mrs Torrence that I would get her check in the mail today."

I looked down the hall and then back to my employee. "Oh ... sure." I said reluctantly, following her into her office. She made small talk and I tried to not show how anxious I was to leave, but as soon as I had it signed off I hurried to Nikki's office. But she wasn't there. She had already left for lunch. I thought about calling her and then I stopped. I just stopped right in my tracks.

No. I wasn't going to apologize. Why should I? She didn't apologize for having unprotected sex with some guy she'd just met. I stormed back into my office and slammed the door shut.

Much later, the office phone was ringing and I blinked. I had just been sitting, staring off into space for the last fifteen minutes. Damn, I needed to get my head straight. I picked up.

"Hello?"

"Toi?" Shit; it was Mom.

"Why you not call? I thought you call after doctor visit? You lose cell phone?"

"Ah ... no. I'm sorry, Mom, things just got a little crazy."

"Crazy? What wrong, Toi?"

"Nothing."

"Son. What is wrong? Talk to me?"

I cleared my voice. Why is it that talking to your mother makes you want to instantly start bawling and to climb up into her lap like you are just two years old again? But I didn't start bawling, I swallowed back everything that I was feeling.

"We had the ultrasound and got to hear the baby's heartbeat."

"Ah." She said happily.

"And the technician told us that the baby was sixteen weeks developed. Problem is, Mom ... Nikki and I have only been together thirteen and a half weeks."

There was a long quiet. "I see. Where is Nikki?"

I shrugged. "At lunch I guess." Or maybe back in her office or home. I didn't know and found that I didn't care.

"And where are you?"

I sighed and looked out the window. "In my office." She called here, right? But I knew where she was going with this.

"Ganbatte. Why are you not with her?"

"Mom ... I just need space. I need to think."

"Nikki is scared and hurting, too. You need to be with her."

"Mom ... "

"Toi, listen to me. Nikki is the same woman that you loved a week ago. She is going through this same process with you, finding out that she is pregnant, making plans for the future with you, and then finding out this news, too. She didn't do this on purpose. This is before you. This is Nikki and if you love her then you love everything about her ... including her baby." I felt tears sting my eyes.

"I don't know if ... if I want to do that, Mom." It hurt to say it, but it was the truth.

"Then ... you never really loved her." Her voice was suddenly chilly ... and strangely there was not a bit of a Japanese accent to it. "Just be man enough to tell her that it's over." My heart caved at the idea of that.

"I don't want that either."

"Go to her and tell her you love her."

"Yeah." Tears dripped from my eyes. "Yeah."

NIKKI

Lunch for me was a walk outside to clear my head. I was wearing a pair of Loubitin pumps, so not the smartest thing to do. I didn't want to cry and for everyone at the office to see the tell-tale signs of my tears because I had raccoon eyes. So instead of focusing on what hurt, I focused on what made me so angry; like how Tony was a jackass.

One kind word, one show of support would have meant the world to me. Even if he had continued with the whole needing to think and needing space, at least I wouldn't be sitting here in this turmoil wondering what he is feeling, at least I would know that he ...

Did he still love me?

Even having to wonder that almost took the breath out of me and I stopped walking for a moment. I couldn't even imagine my life without Tony in it. I placed my hand on my belly. My baby was in there. Mine. Regardless of Tony or Dean. And yeah, I would get through this no matter the outcome because I had this wondrous little one to consider.

I went back to the office, a little less anxious, but still stinging from my meeting with Tony. So imagine my surprise when I saw Tony sitting there waiting for me. I closed the door slowly and decided not to speak. Sometimes there was a time to speak and sometimes there was a time to listen.

He stood up quickly. He looked like hell, just in the short span of time since I'd last seen him.

"Nikki ... I am so sorry, baby. I am so sorry that I haven't been around. I'm sorry for counseling you about Durdak. I'm sorry." He watched me with an open expression. "I know that I was being a jerk." He hurried to me and took my hand. "I love you. I love all of you, your passion, your anger. I love your baby. Regardless ... " He stared deeply into my eyes. "Regardless of whether it's my child or not, I love this baby because it's you."

My arms went around him so fast that I think that he flinched wondering if I was going to haul off and hit him. But no, I hugged him like he was my lifeline. I felt him sigh as his arms went around me.

"I didn't want you to apologize." I said, my voice trembling so I guess I was crying again. "I just wanted to know that you were still with me. I'm the one that's sorry! I have you in this situation and ... I'm so sorry-"

He pulled back, arms still around me. "I don't care. That was before US."

"You ... you love the baby?"

He smiled. And it was genuine. "Does it really matter if my blood runs through this baby's body? I'm still going to be this baby's father. He or she is still going to be baby Yakamoto because I still intend to marry his mother."

My knees trembled and hot and cold waves went through me. He'd proposed! It wasn't a 'will you marry me?' But there was no need to even ask that

question because I would! Will! I'm going to marry
Toi Yakamoto! I hugged him again and this time he
picked me up and swung me into a slow circle before
re-depositing me lightly onto my feet.

"We're going to have to tell people-" I began but
he placed his lips onto mine and kissed me. My body
turned to liquid. Afterwards he looked at me. What
had I been saying?

"I have to run an errand. I have to go to Isadore
Durdak's home and give her the re-fi check directly.
Afterwards, I'm going to need to spend a relaxing
evening in the arms of my woman. Do you think we
can make that happen?"

I nodded solemnly. "You ... you have to
apologize to her?"

"I need to grovel a bit. But this is a good day for
it. At least I got practice." He tried to smile but it fell
way short.

"Can I go with you?" He gave me a surprised
look.

"But-"

"Please?"

His expression cleared. "Of course, if you want. I
suppose we should head out now." He went back to
his office to let his secretary know where he was going
and to lock up. I made a quick phone call to
underwriting to let them know about an error on
closing papers for another client and then we drove
off together leaving my car behind.

He closed his hands over mine. "I'm not sure
why you want to do this, Nikki."

"Because you have to if I don't." He gave me a quick look and then I felt him briefly squeeze my hand.

We were at Mrs Durdak's house within minutes and I was appalled at what I saw. The house was in such disrepair that I was ashamed for her. Hopefully she would use some of the money for home repairs because the neighborhood was rather affluent and the normal upkeep was impeccable. Didn't she have family? I didn't expect her to climb a ladder and fix the fallen shingle or paint the rickety front porch, but someone in her family should have taken the initiative.

With a grim expression on my face Tony and I went to the front door and rang the bell. It was probably not functioning so Tony knocked.

For seventy-two, Mrs Durdak sure moved well. She was at the door in a flash of colorful cloth. She was wearing a casual yet expensive burnt orange and brown pants suit. It made the older woman look about ten years younger than her age, which she was proud to tell you.

She gave Tony an up and down look and when she saw me she actually snorted. Tony and I exchanged looks.

"Mrs Durdak. I'm Toi Yakamoto. I wanted to come by and bring you the refinance check personally-"

"I know who you are. Come in then." She held the door wide for us to enter. I was blown away. The shambles on the outside did not match the inside.

This house was magnificent; a bit austere for my tastes, it still was well maintained and richly decorated.

"You have a lovely home." I said honestly.

"Thank you. I like nice things." She had an uncharacteristically haughty look about her. Well she was obviously pissed about being denied in the first place.

Tony was staring at a curio cabinet. "Your collection of Lladro is beautiful."

Her severe expression began to soften. "Thank you. I've been a collector for decades." Tony's feet moved to the cabinet and Mrs Durdak joined him. "Ahh, you like the Asian one. That is springtime in Japan."

"It's beautiful. I have the Hina dolls."

"Both of them?" Mrs Durdak's brow went up.

"Yes, both the Emperor and the Empress."

"I'm impressed. Not many men collect Lladro."

"I'm not a true collector. I just see pieces that I like."

"I have a bronzed figural Geisha lamp circa 1870. It doesn't match anything in my house but it's beautiful."

Tony's eyes lit up. "May I see it?"

She actually smiled. "Certainly, my boy." Wow, Tony was good at this type of thing. Mrs Durdak had already pretty much dismissed me. Well, I may not be quite the 'people' person that Tony was but it didn't mean that I didn't have heart or didn't care. I followed them to a sitting room that was very nicely decorated in antique, yet comfortable chairs. On the side table set a black, ugly lamp with a birdhouse sitting on top of the Geisha's up stretched hands.

"Wow, that is magnificent." Tony said with true awe in his voice. I tried to see it through his eyes … and yet all I could see was an ugly lamp. She went around the room and pointed out other antique pieces. Each item, Tony looked on with appreciation and true interest. After fifteen minutes in the room I was getting tired. I sat down in one of the chairs and Mrs Durdak gave me a sharp look.

"Chile, that chair is not made for big girls. It will collapse on you like matchsticks!" I jumped up and blushed. I saw Tony press his lips together in order to hide that he was two seconds from laughing. I ignored him.

"I'm sorry. Mrs Durdak, I wanted to come here with Toi so that I could explain why I denied your loan."

Tony gave me a dubious look but did not speak.

The older woman pursed her lips. "Oh, I know why you denied my loan. I'm used to colored girls like you that can't stand to see another black get ahead. I've had to deal with trifling Negroes like yourself all of my life!"

My mouth fell open. What the fuck?! Even Tony took on a look of shock at her severe words.

"Mrs Durdak, Miss Mason is not that person. I can assure you that your race had nothing to do with why the loan was denied."

"Then why? Why did the whites always give me loans but the one black I come up against denies me?!"

I couldn't even speak, I was so outdone. I just walked out of the room and towards the front door. I wasn't going to apologize to this woman. Let her deal with the consequences of her own ignorance.

"Nikki!" Tony gripped my arm. "Tell her! You came here to tell her so don't leave without doing it!"

Mrs Durdak watched us silently. Reluctantly I turned towards her. I narrowed my eyes.

"Mrs Durdak, I'm going to be frank with you. Since you were blunt with me, I'm just going to be the same."

"Do it. I got my check, at this stage of the game I've got what I wanted. You can be as blunt as you want."

I didn't like this woman quite as much as I had three weeks ago. Yet she did remind me of someone I knew, myself.

"Mrs Durdak. You are seventy-two years old and you look ten years younger than that." She smirked at me. "But you are still getting older. One day you may not want to live in this big house. Maybe you will face some unfortunate accident that could cause you to move ... to a condo or something. I don't know." Tony had already closed his eyes in horror at my words.

"What I'm saying is that if you had to leave this house, sell it, you'd still have the rest of the loan to pay off. If I bought this house I'd buy it for what it is valued at, no more. But what you're receiving a loan for is more than the value of this house. If you sold it, you'd still be essentially paying off this loan. Bottom line. You would still owe my company over fifty thousand dollars even AFTER your house sold. And that is if anyone would buy it. In this economy and with the exterior condition you would have to unload this at a very reduced price."

Her eyes flashed at me, both fire and something else. "I'm not going to sale my house, Miss Mason. So that won't be an issue for me. I intend to live out the rest of my years here."

"Great. Then it doesn't matter if you pay us an extra fifty thousand to do it!" I opened the front door and stormed down the stairs. Damnit, what had I just done? I'd let my anger get in the way and I'd yelled at a customer and basically told her that my company was nothing more than a bunch of crooks. Shit! I was going to be in so much trouble.

Tony returned to the car about five minutes later. I studied his expression. He'd come here to make things right and instead I'd made them worse. He didn't get into the car, but came around to the passenger side. I rolled down my window.

"Babe, congratulations. Mrs Durdak doesn't want the loan and she wants to talk to you." I looked up to the doorway to see the older woman standing there watching. I got out of the car and went back into the house. Mrs Durdak took my elbow and led me back inside. This time we went into a kitchen. It was a little dated but seemed very comfortable and was neat and tidy.

"Your man told me off pretty good." I flashed Tony a look but his expression remained passive.

"My man ... um-?"

"I know he's your man. It's in the way that you feel being in the same room with each other, even if you don't think that your face or manner shows it, it really does. But the point is I jumped to a conclusion. Sit down." Tony and I sat on red velvet covered barstools while Mrs Durdek went into the refrigerator for iced tea.

"Do you like sweet tea?"

"Yes, ma'am." We both replied. She poured us all large glasses of tea and then sat down and watched us.

"I pride myself on being a smart, educated woman. You know, smart and educated aren't synonymous. In my life I've met many people who were very educated and well versed in their respective fields ... but in some cases, they were some of the dumbest-assed people I've met!" I hid a smile. "I never wanted to be that person, but I think that I am. Miss Mason, please accept my apology for what I said earlier. In my attempt to pay down my bills, I've had several over-sights. I suppose I wilfully tried not to see the obvious.

"Mr Yakamoto told me that you are a real estate agent. I lied when I said that I wanted to die in this house. I can't think of anything that I'd despise more ... dying in this hellish reminder of a life that I no longer live."

I glanced at Tony curiously. "Yes, ma'am. I have a real estate license."

"Do you think that you can help me sell this house for enough money to pay off my bills and to get situated in a nice little condo? I'd like to have a yard because I love tending to my flowers and herbs."

I smiled. "I would love to help you. This is a beautiful house and with a little work it could sell for enough to pay off your previous loans and your debt and perhaps even enough to place a small down payment on a condo. I actually know of several condos that would give you the space of a single family, as well as a private yard … "

When Tony and I were back in the car and on our way back to the office I was almost trembling with the thrill of helping instead of hurting someone. I gave Tony a worried look.

"Mr Milton is going to be pissed."

"Yes. Especially when he finds out that Mrs Durdak is going to file another complaint against the company with the Better Business Bureau for predatory mortgage practices." There was a strange, peaceful look on his face. He reached out and touched my hand.

"I'm proud of you Nikki."

"I guess this means that I get a lowered evaluation."

But it turned out to be worse than that.

We both got fired.

TONY

When we returned to the office, I went straight to Richard Milton's office and handed him back the check. I was honest when I informed him that Mrs Durdak had declined our services. I was frank when I mentioned that she would not be removing her report to the BBB but would be, in fact, filing a new one. I never mention Nikki at all in this. He did.

With a face that was angry and beet red, he glared at me. "It has come to my attention that there has been an indiscretion in the company. Are you and Nikkita Mason involved in a relationship of a romantic nature?"

"We're engaged." I said. That surprised him completely. Evidently he, as well as all of the people in the office, had known that there was something going on between Nikki and I (silly us to think that no one could see that we were completely in love with each other), but I suppose he figured that it was little more than a seedy office affair … like the one that he has been having with my secretary Debbie.

"As a direct supervisor of Nikkita, the relationship violates company policy. Clearly you are in a position to exercise influence over her pay and awards. I don't know what you were thinking when you embarked on this misguided fling-"

"I'm ENGAGED." I spoke almost casually. "How is that misguided, or a fling?"

He wasn't inclined to answer the question. "I have no choice but to terminate yours and Nikkita's employment with the company."

I unbuttoned my jacket. "I see. Well draw up the severance package. I'll sign the forms in your office. I don't want them mailed to me. I also request my last check to be received by hand, here in your office and not by mail. How soon will you be able to have these things for me?"

"Uh … I … " he stammered. "You seemed to be prepared for this." My lip twisted.

"I don't want to work here anymore. I'm not happy doing this job anymore. But I wouldn't have gotten my severance package if I had quit, now would I?" His face began to move from beet red to pale. "Richard, it was you that challenged me to decide whether I wanted to live on principal or on regrets. When I handed the woman I love a reprimand for something that she didn't deserve, I realized that I was incapable of living with regrets. So yeah … I'm out of here. Just tell me when I can sign my departure papers."

He didn't answer for a long time. "I'll have them ready for you tomorrow." He finally answered. I stood and re-buttoned my jacket.

"Richard, despite everything, I appreciate the chance you gave me at this company. I'll be back tomorrow to collect my things."

I went to Nikki's office. She gave me a fearful look knowing that I was going to be meeting with Richard to give him the unfortunate news. I winked at her. "Let's go, beautiful. We need to start looking for new jobs."

NIKKI

I placed my hand on my belly. I was only five months pregnant now but my belly swelled enough for my condition to be unmistakable. When I told my Mom and Daddy they were shocked. They liked Tony, but maybe they thought that I'd move on to a black man. Then Mom said that it was going to be the prettiest baby. And when she said that, it seemed that it was all that anyone could talk about; how pretty a black and Asian child would be.

I couldn't bring myself to mention the fact that there was a big chance that the baby would not be Tony's. If that happened then I could explain then. Still, everyone would think that I was a cheater. Daddy was still looking at me with some concern.

"You two are unemployed. How are you going to do this?"

"Daddy, we will get through this. Tony got a huge severance package-"

"That's him. What about you?" His statement was true. I got no severance package because I hadn't been with the company at least a year. I was collecting unemployment and I'd get paid helping Mrs Durdak sell her house, but after that I didn't know. I told Daddy that Tony's insurance would be in position for a year after separation and that when

151

we got married I'd be on his policy so that would cover the baby's birth.

Daddy just shook his head and didn't say anything else. Well hell, this wasn't the dream I'd had either! Thankfully Tony was off playing basketball with his friend's and couldn't witness this exchange. He had been slow to put out feelers to other mortgage companies. When I asked him what his plans were, he just got a thoughtful look on his face and responded that it would have to be something he enjoyed. Me, I decided to hold off on looking for a job until after the baby was born. I simply didn't want to get turned down from a promising company because I was in the last stages of pregnancy.

I went home, happy to be away from Daddy's worrisome stare and Mom's fussing about the baby's looks. Wu-Tang greeted me happily and I spent a few moments rubbing her soft fur. Tony had given up his condo and had moved in with me. For the present his nicer, but more contemporary furniture was in storage. I loved living with this thoughtful man. He cooked and cleaned up after himself. He was neat and considerate of the fact that he shared a space with me. In turn, I made sure to offer him a place where he could feel was his as well as mine.

But I wanted a house. I wanted our own home and a place for the baby that didn't include a crib in our bedroom ... of course I needed to be Mrs Yakamoto first and we were at an impasse on wedding planning. Tony liked doing everything classy and he was talking a boatload of money, which

I couldn't see us spending since we weren't currently employed. Tony always said for me not to worry about money but how could I not?

I decided to lie down for a nap until Tony came home and then maybe we'd decide on what to do for dinner. Sometime later I heard someone bamming on the front door. I jumped up almost before I'd completely awakened. But even before I got to the front door I heard Tony arguing with someone. Then I heard a voice that I didn't ever want to hear again; Dean's. Oh shit. There was only one reason that he'd be here.

I opened the door. Tony was wearing basketball shorts and a sweaty t-shirt. He hadn't showered at the gym or changed. His normally stylish hair lay flatly, almost long enough to touch his shoulders. It hid most of his face—not a bad thing since he was so angry. There was a dark, sinister look in his eyes as he jabbed a finger into Dean's chest.

"No! You're not going in there. You're not talking to her-"

Dean's face was equally twisted and dark. He was easily six feet three inches so he towered over Tony. He was the type of guy that would turn any woman's head; chocolate skin, goatee, shaved head and a body that was sculptured perfection. He also was a lame excuse for a man. He never paid much attention to me. I wasn't Nikki, I was the girl he was boning. Or I was that person to makes excuses to for why he didn't come home when he said he would. He played video games for hours and hours, he always tried to tell me how to manage my life, my finances, he even once told me to get rid of my 401k because people were always trying to go broke saving for the end of their lives when they should be devoting their efforts to enjoying NOW. I think that was the last time that I cared to listen to anything he had to say.

Dean's eyes swung to me belly and he suddenly had a horror stricken look on his face. "Jesus ... you are pregnant." His eyes met mine. "Is it mine?" Tony was quiet then and so was I. Dean gave me a look of utter disbelief. "You really wouldn't have told me, would you?"

"What are you doing here?" I asked. It was the only thing I could say, although the answer was fairly obvious.

"I needed to see for myself. Tony says it's his but I'm asking you. Whose baby is this?"

I gave Tony a perplexed look. How had we gotten here, like this?

I sighed. "Come inside. I think we all need to talk." Tony did not look happy but he followed us into the house.

TONY

Knowing that I was unemployed didn't stress me out as much as it would others. I had a fat bank account, a 401k to fall back on and time to decide what career path I wanted to take. Nikki wasn't quite as relaxed. I'm not sure why she was so stressed, other than that she is just a naturally stressed out individual. Pregnancy and unemployment hasn't helped. But money is not an issue so I wish she wouldn't be so anxious.

She had decided to reveal all news to her family in baby steps. First she told them that we were unemployed and after that died down she announced our engagement and today she is going to tell her people that she is pregnant. I wisely declined to attend that particular revelation because I had told her to tell them immediately. But she claimed to know and understand her parent's so here we are telling them nearly a month after we'd discovered it.

Once I stopped being a dumb-ass and I let Nikki know that I wanted her AND her baby regardless of who had fathered it, our lives seemed to return to a comfortable routine. Doctor visits, baby shopping, and just more time for us to reunite as a couple. Pregnancy sex is very good and because of the hormones, she is insatiable.

I don't think about the fact that the baby might be born looking like her and Dean instead of her and me. I don't think of baby names because there may not be a little Iyoki. I just think about holding this little newborn in my arms and knowing that when he or she looks at me, I am the only Daddy that he or she knows.

I don't even despise Dean as much as I thought I would. Recently, after going to his place for an online HALO tournament in which he and I were on the same team, Dean came up to me exclaiming how good I'd played for a newbie. We'd had fun and he apologized for how our friendship had declined. I was one step away from telling him not to apologize to me but to Nikki before I realized that I didn't want this fool even knowing that there was a baby that might be his. I couldn't stop thinking that he might be stuck in my life forever ... or for the next eighteen years. So I shook his hand and told him that it was water under the bridge.

Having that change of attitude toward each other somewhat rekindled our friendship. And though he and I aren't as tight as the other guys and I are, we are cool. At least until Jay got that phone call from his mother during our weekly basketball game at the rec center.

We were in the locker after another good game. Someone had mentioned getting some beers and Dean had said that we'd just sweated away like a thousand calories and he wanted to drink them right back up? We were in our thirties and pretty conscious that it now actually took work to stay in shape and to look good. Even Budda had dropped enough weight that he couldn't be called pudgy anymore.

Jay was on his cell checking his messages and I was about to do the same, curious about how Nikki's revelation had gone. But Jay beat me to it. He being Nikki's cousin meant that his mother had already informed him of the baby news. Jay swung around to me with a huge grin on his face.

"You fucking dog!" He yelled happily. "Why the fuck didn't you tell me that you and Nikki were having a baby?!" He jumped on me, thumping me on the back. The other guys turned to me in disbelief.

"T-baby finally impregnated a sister?!" Pac joked.

"Dude, how are you going to keep a secret like that for five damn months?!" Jay laughed. "I didn't even know that you two were together that long!" I don't know why I did it, but my eyes swung to Dean.

He was watching the interaction quietly but then his hand froze as he was unlacing one of his shoes. His eyes met mine and his mouth dropped. He stood up slowly.

"Five months?" The other guys were slapping my back and congratulating me but I kept my eyes on Dean. "That's pretty close, T."

I saw him begin doing some calculations in his head. Then his expression cleared and he looked at me again. "Am I the father?"

The room got instantly quiet and I mean you could hear a pin drop. We aren't the only guys in the locker but absolutely no one said a word.

157

"No, Dean." I said angrily. "You aren't."

"Oh you are a fucking liar." He said in dawning realization. "You were never a good liar! Your tell is showing right now!"

For a moment I thought he meant tail, and then I realized that I had blinked too many times. That was my tell. Shit.

Jay looked back and forth from one to the other of us. "No..." He was blown over. "No no no no no. Dean! You and Nikki?!"

"Before Nikki and me." I said. "But that-"

"You were fucking my cousin?!" Jay was all up in Dean's face. Jay and Dean are comparable in height so when they pushed off each other's chests it was like two mountains colliding. "Dude, we had a deal. You don't fuck anyone's relative, or anybody we know! And you broke that promise, dude!"

His mouth flew open and he pointed to me. "T has been fucking your cousin! Why aren't you telling this to him?!"

"Because T is a good man. He doesn't fuck over people like you do! You knock my cousin up-"

My eyes practically rolled to the back of my head and I almost blacked out; that is how fast I got mad. "NOBODY KNOCKED UP NIKKI BUT ME! I AM THE FATHER OF THIS BABY!"

Dean pushed past all of us. "I'm going to get to the bottom of this!" I hurried out of the locker room after him.

"Where the fuck do you think you're going?! No! Don't even think about going to Nikki's place!" We were pushing and shoving each other and then we were outside. He went to his truck and I jumped into my car. Then we raced to the apartment. I'm not completely sure how we didn't wreck or take out a highway full of people, but he reached the apartment first, his truck partially up on the curb.

I pulled up behind him and he was already banging on the door to be let in. I grabbed him and pulled him away. "Back off, dude, or I will kick your ass!" He smacked my hand away and pushed me hard enough to cause me to stumble backwards.

"Fuck off, T! You knew all along!"

"There ain't nothing to know!" Then Nikki opened the door, looking like she'd just awakened from a nap. And he asked her. And she didn't tell him that it was mine. I thought that's what we had agreed; this baby was mine, not anyone else's regardless of whose sperm had impregnated her ovum. Dean didn't have to be here when I was going to step up to the plate regardless!

"Come in. We need to talk about this." I gave her an incredulous look. Why did we need to talk about this? But I didn't say anything, unsure of what might leave my mouth. We went inside and I tried hard not to pace.

"Nikki? Could this be my baby?"

I saw her cross her arms in an almost defensive motion. "It could be."

Dean just nodded. After a moment he took in a deep breath. "That night I broke through the condom …"

159

Nikki's eyes flitted to mine and then she nodded. "Maybe."

My breathing was coming in shallow spurts. I wanted to punch something, but why? This was before me. We should be able to discuss this in an adult manner ... except that I wanted to rip Dean's cock off and shove it up his ass!

"Why didn't you tell me?! Were you ever going to tell me?!"

"I didn't tell you because I didn't know until very recently myself. And considering that the last time I'd seen you, it was with you calling me a bitch, I wasn't all that anxious to seek you out!"

Dean's jaw clenched. "I'm sorry for that. I mean, you dumped me and I was just being a child over it. But this is so much more important, Nikki. I mean ... don't you see that?"

She nodded. "Tony and I just found out ourselves a little less than a month ago. We're trying to deal with it as well. And when the baby comes and if it turns out that you are the father, then yes, I would have let you know." I looked at her, not realizing that this was the plan.

Dean relaxed a bit more. "Well I want to be there for you, Nikki, during this process-"

"That's not necessary." I said tightly. "She has a fiancée-"

"That doesn't have a job." My mouth parted.

"Dean!" Nikki snapped. "We are not struggling-"

"But a man works for his family."

"And a man doesn't come to a woman's house drunk, beating on her door and calling her names! So fuck you, Dean!" I said angrily.

"No, fuck you, Tony! I apologized for that and I see that you didn't even come back and tell her that I did! I mean, I know that she didn't want to see me. But you could have told her!"

I scowled. "So now you know. We'll keep in touch." I went to the door and opened it for him.

He and Nikki exchanged looks and she nodded slightly for him to leave. I hated that small show of intimacy. He headed to the door, pausing before he was outside where I could slam it loudly after him.

"Nikki, I want you to know that I'm very sorry for how everything went down. And despite how it appeared at the end, the brief time we spent with each other was good. I know I was an ass. But I hope you can accept my apology." He glared at me. "If you need anything; money, whatever, call me."

I held my breath and counted to ten. I got to seven before he was out of the door and it was slammed and locked behind him.

"T how did he find out-?"

"Why in the hell did you invite him in?!"

She gave me a look that seemed to say, 'I know you didn't just yell at me.'

I returned a look that said, 'Yes I did!'

"Why are you mad at me?" She asked and that simple question diffused me.

"I-I don't know."

"Well figure it out!" She stormed out of the room and back to the bedroom where she promptly slammed the door.

I did what she said, and I took a few minutes to figure it out. Then I tentatively opened the bedroom door where she was lying in bed on her side and staring at the wall.

"Hi baby." I said.

She glanced at me. "Hi." Her voice was shaky and it crushed me to know that she was so close to tears.

"I'm sorry."

She sat up and looked at me. "Tony, how many times do I have to apologize to you? I'm sorry that this happened." Tears gushed from her eyes. "I'm devastated that I'm doing this to you." I went to the bed and pulled her into my arms.

"Baby, come here. I don't want you to apologize. I don't need that." She buried her head in my chest. "Just don't cry, okay?" I tilted her chin upward and wiped away her tears. We just stared at each other. I placed my fingertips onto her belly. I felt the baby in there moving and I smiled and then she did as well.

"You're a wonderful man." She whispered. She placed her fingertips on my eyes and I closed them. She traced the crease where my lids joined, following it lightly, and when her fingers moved to touch my nose I opened my eyes again. Her hands moved to my hair and she swept her fingers through the strands.

My finger's moved to her breasts and I stroked her nipple feeling it pucker through the material of her bra. I cupped her breast in my hand, testing the increased weight and she groaned softly when my thumb circled the hardened flesh of her nipple.

I sighed and urged her back onto the bed. She laid back watching me with love and trust. I slipped off her shirt and unlatched her bra and then softly I kissed each brown peak. I covered her with my open mouth and carefully drew her breast into my mouth, careful not to tug too hard. She drew in a sharp breath and her back arched.

Sitting up I pushed down her pants and she helped me by kicking them off. I caressed her mound, spreading her wet hot flesh and then stroking her gently and repeatedly until her breath was heavy and strained. She pulled me down to kiss her and I did, stroking her as I did. Her hips rose to meet my touch and I looked at her and whispered,

"What do you want me to do?"

"Inside of me. I want you inside of me." She turned to her side. We found that was the easiest way. I came out of my clothes, ready to enter her, which I did carefully, holding her in my arms, her back against me. I lightly pinched her nipples; first one then the other as I rocked gently within her.

She cried out her pleasure with each gentle thrust and I slipped my fingers between her crease and lightly pinched her clit. She grunted indelicately and began gyrating her hips rapidly, forcing me to increase my pace. But I was not going to be as hard as she wanted. That scared me though she assured me that I couldn't hurt the baby who was nowhere near her vagina. Maybe she was right but I made sure to pull my pumping hips.

Soon, the sound of Nikki's steady groans picked up in tempo and volume. I felt my balls tighten and rise and then I was cumming along with her. Trying to control my own orgasm only caused it to feel that much better and I gripped her hips roughly, holding her in place while I continued to pump into her. After a moment the last jolt of electricity slammed into me and I cried out cumming violently yet gently into her.

Afterwards, Nikki hummed contentedly and I showered her neck and shoulders with kisses. Before she fell asleep I whispered into her ear.

"Nikki?"

"Hmmm?"

"You and Dean ... " she turned her head to look at me.

"What?"

"Did you ... did you always use ... um protection?" Because she hadn't with me. She was on the pill with me. Maybe I shouldn't ask, but it was the thing that I needed to know.

She sat up in bed and turned to me, her face calm. "Always." I swallowed. "I always used protection with him. The condom broke once." She touched my face. "T, I've made love to men without using protection before. But the thing is; I made love with them. I was never in love with Dean and we always used a condom."

I nodded, ashamed that I'd even asked. But I felt better knowing.

NIKKI

Mrs Durdak's house had almost gone through a complete transformation in just two short months. I was doing the final walk through before the first open house. Tony swept into the living room wearing dirty jeans and an even dirtier t-shirt.

"Baby!" I exclaimed. "You are funky!"

"I know but you wanted the fountain working, right? I finally got it going and it looks great."

"Oh wow!" I hurried out the door. Mrs Durdak was already standing there looking at it with pleasure. She clapped her hands when she saw me.

"It's beautiful." She did a slow spin. "Everything is beautiful." And it was. The yard was impeccable as usual, and the house now matched it. There was new vinyl siding, the roof had been repaired and the gutters replaced, there were new shutters and the porch had been repaired and painted and it now looked great.

I looked at Tony proudly. He had orchestrated much of the work himself and where he couldn't do it himself, he had called in some favors and traded in some of the comps that he'd gotten from work in exchange for material. My cousin and their friends had helped out and instead of hanging out at the rec center once a week they spent time here getting things in order. Mrs Durdak was so happy to have the guys present. She called them boys and cooked for them and they loved being spoiled by her. Dean, of course didn't show up. T mentioned that he was lying low and had declined any invitation in which they had to be in each other's presence.

I kissed T even though he was funky and dirty. I was so proud of him. We'd all worked so hard. Mrs Durdak placed a kiss on both of our cheeks and then returned to the house.

"Okay, smelly man, go back home and get changed." He swatted my ass and then hurried to the car. Several people were standing outside of the fence and I ambled over and opened it even though we still had another twenty or twenty-five minutes before it was actually scheduled to show.

It felt good to show the house. It was beautiful and received lots of ooohs and ahhs. It didn't hurt that Mrs Durdak was a collector and several people recognized her antiques. I had told her not to get her hopes up too high on this first showing as the economy made it difficult for people to afford a major purchase, not to mention that it was much harder to qualify for a loan. Generally this first showing was for real estate agents to get an idea of what we had.

But at the end of the evening she had two offers on the large house; both from neighbors willing to finish up with any updates and repairs. Tears were in Mrs Durdak's eyes when I gave her the news. I worried that she had regrets and might want to back out of selling but that wasn't it.

"How soon can I move? I can't wait to get into my condo!" She had fallen in love with the very first place I'd shown her. I knew it would be a perfect match for her. She covered my hands.

"I want to do something special for you and your man. I know you two are trying to save money. And I feel so bad about you two not having jobs."

"For the millionth time, that wasn't your fault. Neither of us wanted to be there anymore."

"Yes, I know but still … I want to do something nice for you. I want to hold the wedding here at the house … well that is; if you can do it before it sells."

I gave her a surprised look, not realizing that she had heard our concerns about the how much to spend on a wedding. And she did have the perfect house for an outdoor wedding. And as things stood we didn't have any place booked and had no hopes of getting anything nice if we wanted to be married before the baby's birth. And of course, she was right, we wanted to save money and were just planning a very private affair.

I hugged her close. "I'll speak to Tony about it. This house would be lovely for a wedding."

Mrs Durdak smiled. She was doing that a lot lately. "It would be nice to send my house off with a bang."

Not even two weeks later, she, my mother and Mrs Y organized a beautiful wedding in the back yard of Mrs Durdak's home. It was a private affair but still had nearly 100 guests including family, friends as well as well-wishers from our former job. Yes, people from the job have been contacting us telling us how much we were missed and how things have changed without Tony's management. There was even talk of an investigation by the FDIC.

It's no stretch that Tony and I decided on a wedding that was a fusion of African-American and Asian. The music of Nujabes drifted softly over the speakers; an artist that mixed traditional Asian music with hip-hop. I saw Mrs Y holding a glass of champagne and dancing in a beautiful manner to the soft music. Mrs Y brought tears to my eyes because she treated me like a daughter throughout the wedding preparations ... as well as before — back when she had first discovered that the baby might not be Tony's.

She showed up at the house early one morning and told me that it was time I learned to make hotpot. I was surprised to see her at the house. I had chickened out of the previous two Sunday dinners, feigning fatigue. So when I saw her at my doorstep I was more than a little nervous. But she didn't even mention the parentage of the baby — not even in that sly way that she had of broaching an off limit topic.

We went to a local Asian market and my eyes were so busy scanning all of the strange packaging that I didn't realize that I had become the center of attention. Several older Asian women were staring at me in a mix of awe and confusion. I looked over at

Mrs Y who was watching me proudly. She spoke in sharp Japanese to the group of spectators.

In unison I heard them all sigh. "Awww." Mrs Y just watched me with pride before finally speaking in her familiar, choppy English. "Nikki these the ladies from my cultural group. We meet on Saturday, talk, play mahjong, eat and drink tea." Then Mrs Y placed her hands on my belly and I grinned. She was showing me off to her friends. It made me feel so special, it was the first time that she made me cry but it wouldn't be the last time. She was so accepting of the baby that I began to wonder how she knew things about this baby before me. So buying into the entire supernatural-Asian thing, one day I asked her if the baby was Tony's. We'd never talked about this. She never treated the baby as if it wasn't her grandchild. I thought maybe she knew something that I didn't.

Mrs Y poured me a cup of tea before answering. "I don't know." She said plainly.

"Oh." I felt both disappointed and stupid.

She gave me a long look. "Nikki, I knew you were pregnant. The signs are clear if you know what to look for. It's not mysticism. I don't know if the father is Tony. I just know that as long as you are my daughter then this baby is my grandchild." That was the second time that she caused me to cry.

I told Tony that I wanted to dress in traditional Japanese attire for our wedding. I wanted to do it for a lot of reasons, to pay tribute to both Tony and his heritage, to give back to Mrs Y and because I was frankly too big to fit comfortably into anything but a

Japanese kimono. Mrs Y was so surprised that this time it was me that made her cry. She insisted on making my white shiromuku, and Tony's black montsuki.

They were beautiful. I know that I'm supposed to be the gorgeous one but when I saw T standing under a real rose trellis wearing the traditional black kimono and pants I almost lost my breath. His hair was long enough to tie back and he stood there so straight, and I knew that it was all for me; for us.

Of course, when he saw me he seemed to be doing the same thing. It was a true union. We had the pastor from church actually perform the service. And then in an act of humor, Mrs Durdak and my cousin Jay placed a broom across the velveteen red carpet for us to jump over. Tony and I laughed so hard. I held my tummy and then tentatively jumped over the broom. Everyone cheered for us and I felt like I was on top of the world.

After the wedding we had a Japanese reception called a kekkon hiroen. And then we all lined up and did the electric slide; what wedding would be complete without it? Even Mr and Mrs Y joined in.

On top of all that Mrs Durdak had done for us, as a wedding present she gave us the antique Geisha lamp that Tony had admired.

"Mrs Durdak … " He tried to hand it back to her. "This is too much, I can't accept this-"

She made a hmph sound. "There really is no place for it in my condo. If you don't take it, it will go in storage and then I'll just will it to you when I die."

Tony's chocolate eyes twinkled. "In that case, thank you! I absolutely love this piece." He kissed her and that seemed to make her day.

It was closing in on midnight before we went off for our honeymoon; which was back to our apartment with Wu-Tang and a movie. There was absolutely no place that I would have rather been.

TONY

Nikki sighed and I played particular attention to the tight knots around her neck and shoulders. I gave her a massage every night because at this stage of the pregnancy she was fairly uncomfortable. Mostly it was her feet and legs but tonight it was her shoulders and neck.

"What's wrong, babe?"

She peeked at me. "Why do you think there's something wrong?"

"Because your neck feels like a heavy weight boxer's."

She sighed again and then rolled over and struggled to sit up with me helping her. "Baby a house just came on the market. I know I shouldn't but I've fallen in love with it. You know how you see something when you're not even looking for it, and it's everything that you ever want?"

I gave her a knowing look. "I know that feeling exactly. It's the feeling I had when I first saw you."

She smiled slowly. "Thank you." She leaned over and kissed me.

"Tell me about this house."

She sighed and stood up, stretching. "It is so perfect. It's like … US." She grinned. "There's a real Japanese garden in back, with a koi pond and a small bridge! Can you believe that?" But then her

173

expression dropped. "But it's a Frank Lloyd Wright and you know what that means; when it goes on the market there's going to be a bidding war."

"Babe, I didn't know that you were anxious to get into a house-"

"No, I'm not. I mean, it's just that this house came out of the blue, and it's in perfect condition. The owner's have retained all of its character. There's a Victorian kitchen with very little update other then appliances! Baby, it's beautiful."

"Well I think we should make an offer. I mean I'd like to see it first but-"

"Tony ... we can't get a home loan in this economy; not without jobs."

I wasn't used to hearing those words. They were foreign to my ears. The idea that I couldn't buy something because I had no job almost floored me. I had been thinking about all of the money I had tied to me, but when it came down to it, I was still an unemployed man.

I had never realized that until just now.

"I want to see the house." I said finally.

She nodded. "I'll set up an appointment."

Nikki was able to set the appointment to see the house that same evening. The owners were a gay couple that loved the house but needed to move out of state fairly quickly. When we drove up the driveway my heart was beating a mile a minute. There was something about it that felt like home; from the stone and brick, to the leaded glass windows to the front porch beneath the roofline. I loved it and I hadn't even been inside of it yet.

The owner's took great pride in showing the house. It truly had the wow factor and I couldn't help but to comment on the beautiful woodwork and inset shelving. I asked if it was on the registry and it was.

"We'd like to see it stay. I realize we can't dictate what the new owners will do-"

"What idiot would buy a Frank Lloyd Wright and not keep its character?" I interjected. The two guys looked at each other and then one spoke to Nikki.

"This is your third time here."

She blushed. "I know. I'm sorry. I just really wanted my husband to see it before it went on the market."

"Are you going to put a bid in?"

She shook her head slowly and looked down at the beautifully polished wood floor.

"We'd like to." I answered for her. "But our lives have had a few unexpected changes." Dan, an older white-haired man looked at Nikki's belly.

"Your first?"

Nikki placed her hand over the considerable mound of her belly. I put my arm around her. "Yes." She smiled. "We're newlyweds."

Dan and Jack exchanged looks. "We first moved here in 1987. We were the first gay couple that many of our neighbors had ever met. It took many years but they grew to accept us." Jack said.

"And for the most part, to like us. This is a great neighborhood for an interracial couple. You can say that we've broken them in." Nikki chuckled and then her eyes grew wet.

"Sorry!" She said quickly. "I'm sorry. Hormones." She rushed to the bathroom and Dan and Jack watched me with concern.

I looked after her disappearing form. "Um ... you see the problem is that we both were just let go from our job and neither of us expected to start house hunting until later ... at least I didn't." I admitted.

"Ah, I see." Jack said.

"It's not the money, it's the fact that we aren't currently working ... " I felt like a bum admitting this to them. "Excuse me, I'm going to check on her." I hurried to the bathroom but Nikki was just returning and wiping her eyes with tissue.

"I'm sorry." She apologized. "Look, we'll get out of your hair-"

"Mr and Mrs Yakamoto, put an offer on the house. If you pay what we're asking then we'll sell to you."

"But ... " Nikki stuttered with big surprised eyes. "This house is going to create a bidding frenzy. You're going to get much more then you're asking."

Dan shrugged and went to the kitchen. We followed. "It's never been about the money." He opened the refrigerator and grabbed lemonade. "We had an image of someone that should live in this house. It was someone who would love it enough to cry over it, like we have."

Nikki looked at me quickly. "But ... "

I took her hand. "I told them about the job situation."

"But you have a Real Estate license so actually you're the owner of your own business, right?" Dan said. I stared at Nikki. In actuality it was even more than that. Once Nikki had sold Mrs Durdak's house, then the buyer wanted her to sell theirs. It turned out that there were several other affluent people in the neighborhood in need of a good real estate agent and though she didn't have a shingle over a shop, we had some cards printed with her name on it and Nikki Yakamoto, Real Estate Agent was born.

"It could work."

Nikki jumped up and hugged them both.

Several weeks later my phone rang while I was at the grocery store picking up dinner. Nikki and I were both in a funk. Our house had gone on the market today and there were already several bids on it. I know that I should stop thinking of the craftsman as 'ours' but we both fell in love with it at first sight.

Because I didn't have a job and my name had to appear on the contract, we just weren't eligible to receive a loan. As a matter of fact, if Nikki had applied for the loan herself just a few short weeks earlier—before our wedding, then she might have qualified. But I was the liability; even with my great credit and funds in the bank an unemployed man in America was just that, unemployed.

I felt so bad. I even began dropping my resume at other mortgage companies. It gave me a unique perspective to be on the receiving end of a denial, one that I wouldn't soon forget. I even put in a resume at a massage parlor; when I had only been freelance in the past. I wasn't even sure that I wanted to be a masseuse any longer. Certainly I enjoyed rubbing my wife's body parts but ... Hell, I'd even thought about Nikki and I starting our own real estate business. But I didn't have a real estate license and she did. And besides, that was her passion, not mine.

My phone rang as I was thinking these thoughts. I dug the phone out of my pocket. "Hello."

"Toi Yakamoto?"

"This is Toi." I was hoping that it was a company interested in my resume, though I had only just started putting them out only a few days before.

"Toi, this is Lloyd Cummings." I stopped walking and stood in the middle of the aisle. Lloyd Cummings was the president of my old company.

"Okay."

"Toi. I wanted to talk to you. Do you think that you and I can meet?"

"Talk about what, Mr Cummings?"

"I heard that you were putting in resumes at several other companies." We didn't have a non-compete clause. I hoped they weren't trying to stop me from pursuing a job with perspective competitors.

"Yes."

"I wanted to talk to you about returning to AmeriCom."

My breath froze in my chest.

"You're offering me my old job back?"

"No. I'm offering you Roger Milton's job."

I almost choked. "Roger's no longer with the company?"

"No, he's been let go. Because of him we've been under the scrutiny of the FDIC for mortgage fraud. Toi—"

"Um ... no one calls me Toi. Just Tony."

"Oh, ok, Tony in the past we were a company that cared about the little man but somehow that changed. I take responsibility for not being aware of those changes, or maybe for being an ignorant corporate figurehead. All I saw was the numbers. It took the BBB report to open my eyes. And now the FDIC is investigating. Tony, this company is my baby. And I refuse to let it fail because I didn't know what's what.

"When I asked the people in the know, I was told that you were the person to get back on board. I know that the official paperwork states that you were let go for fraternizing ... and I also know that Roger Milton actually let you go because you weren't pushing through the fraudulent accounts. Tony, I want to thank you. I want to thank you and Nikki Mason-"

"Yakamoto."

"Yakamoto?"

"Yes. Nikki Yakamoto. She's my wife."

"Oh, I didn't realize ... well congratulations-"

I sighed. "Mr Cummings, I appreciate what you're saying, but why would I take on that headache especially with the added scrutiny of the FDIC?"

"Because I have documentation that states you denied a loan that the company tried to push through. Who else would I trust more then you? I'd like to have you and your wife back with the company and I'd make it financially worth your while."

I didn't answer immediately. "Mr Cummings, I need to discuss this with Nikki. Can we talk again later?"

"Certainly. How about we meet at the office tomorrow at noon?"

I hesitated. "I don't know. I'll call you once I've made a decision and we can meet if it's yes."

There was a short pause. "Of course. I'll be waiting for your call." I hung up and swallowed something that tasted like sawdust. Then I immediately called Nikki.

"Baby, you're not going to believe this."

NIKKI

We got the house.

Jack and Dan's real estate agent almost shit her pants when they accepted our lower offer. I ain't gonna lie, I cried during closing and Tony shook his head at me.

"I can't believe you, Nikki. You didn't even cry during our wedding." I kissed him.

"Because I knew I had you, babe."

He smirked.

We got the key and the first thing to get moved into the house was the Geisha lamp from Mrs Durdak and I had to admit that it looked absolutely beautiful in front of the leaded glass bay window.

We then put Wu-Tang on a leash and went walking around our new neighborhood. When we saw our neighbors sitting on their porches or about to get into their cars we always waved and said hello and most of the time that lead to some conversation and we got the opportunity to introduce ourselves. Later, we got take-out Chinese and spent the rest of the day out in the garden where Dan and Jack had left all of the outdoors furniture for us.

"T?" I asked as we rocked in the redwood swing.

"Hmm?" He was in the nearby matching Adirondack chair watching Wu-Tang investigate the garden and making sure she didn't start digging.

181

"You didn't take that job with our old company because you wanted us to get the house, did you?"

"Yeah, I did. But I also took it because I think that I can do something meaningful there. I've learned a lot over the last few months and I'm pretty sure that it will make me a better employer. Are you sure that you don't want to come back to work there?"

I laughed. "I'm positive. If we want to stay married, I think we better not work so close to each other."

"Mmmm. You might be right about that. You don't really follow directions very well."

"Huh? Because I happen to always be right!"

"Whatever, babe. But spanking you in the office is a bit too tempting." I chuckled. Yeah, we really didn't need to work together.

When the sun went down we didn't bother to light the outside torches. We went inside and made love on the mattress and box springs of the bed that we still needed to put together. Besides the lamp it was really the only furniture that we'd brought. We'd already decided that we wouldn't move either of our furniture in since the house demanded something a little more unique than a hodge podge of styles. So we were going to sale our unwanted furniture to a consignment shop and slowly furnish it, choosing each piece with care.

The baby's room was different. We'd already found dark mahogany furniture and T and the boy's planned to paint the baby's room a mellow green, which was a unisex color. Neither of us was interested in learning the sex of the baby … there was more important things to consider.

As I lay in my husband's arms our first night in our first house, I began counting all of my blessings. There was just one last blessing that I wanted.

TONY

I was very excited to get back to work. It wasn't until I returned that I realized just how much I missed my job. On my first day back I brought tea and homemade almond cookies and everyone applauded me. We spent the entire meeting with me reinforcing our purpose and goals. I got them fired up and ready to set a higher standard then we'd had under Richard.

It was Friday and after work I was going to unwind with the guys. Nikki was showing houses and afterwards would then be out having dinner with her Mom and Dad. I worried about her continuing to work even though she was approaching her ninth month of pregnancy. But she didn't see what she was doing as work. I figured that as long as she felt good then I wouldn't worry.

I was singing 'The World is Filled', by Biggie when I stepped out of my car. I had been blasting the music while I drove and despite the fact that I'm sure I looked like the typical wannabe, I couldn't help myself. I liked a lot of the hip-hop that was out now, but there was nothing like the hip hop and rap from back in the day.

"T!"

I heard Dean's call and turned in time to see him getting out of his truck. It had been over a month since I'd last seen him and I wasn't particularly happy to be seeing him now. I waited for him to catch up with me.

"What do you want?"

"Can we talk?"

I sighed and pulled out my cell phone. I dialed Jay who didn't pick up because he was probably already changed. I left him a message. "Look, Dean and I are about to have a discussion so I'll catch up with you all later. Peace out."

Dean was rubbing his goatee. "Did you really just say Peace out?"

I rolled my eyes. "Don't get cute. What do you want?"

"This ... hostility doesn't become you, T-Baby."

I turned away and began walking toward the rec center.

"Wait!" He caught up with me. "Look, when I'm nervous I tell bad jokes. My bad. Do you think we can go somewhere and talk?"

I narrowed my eyes at him. "You ain't packing heat are you?"

"Damn, I'm no killer."

"Well there's a bar around the corner; Fat Cat's. Do you know it?"

"Yeah, I've been there before. I'll meet you there."

He was there before me and had grabbed a table off in a private corner. We were both quiet for a while. I wasn't going to begin, this was his idea not mine.

"How's Nikki?"

My eyes considered him before I answered. "She's doing good."

"I heard you two got married."

I nodded. A waitress came by and asked us if we needed anything. We both ordered beers.

"I'm not going to lie, T. I was surprised that you married her before you found out whose baby she was carrying. I wouldn't have."

"If you loved her you would."

He shook his head. "No. I wouldn't raise another guy's kid. That would be a deal breaker for me." I shrugged not sure where he was going with this. The waitress brought our beers and I waited for him to get to the point.

"Jay was right to warn me away from his cousin. I really thought hard about how people view me. I can't quite say, 'woe is me' when I'm always the asshole in any given situation. Look, I don't have any kids and maybe that would make a difference." He looked at me. "But the thing is, I don't want any. I'm moving out of state."

Now I stared at him. "And if the baby is yours?"

"I'm not going to be a good father." He looked into his beer before taking a drink. "If she draws up the paper work to relinquish my rights, then I'll sign them."

I straightened. "Uh ... Dean, are you sure about this?"

He looked at me. "You already love this baby, don't you?"

"Very much so."

He nodded. "Then I'm sure. Jay was right. You are a good person, T." He reached into his pocket and pulled out a card. "This is how you can get in contact with me. Once the baby is born and the papers are drawn up then call me and I'll sign them."

I took the card. It is what I wanted, but I felt bad. This man would never get to know this wonderful life that was created because he was too selfish and limited. I suppose, more importantly is that he'd given Nikki and I a gift. The gift is that he wouldn't be in our child's life to disappoint him or her.

I reached for my wallet and paid for our beers. "Okay. I'll let her know." He nodded without looking at me and I headed out of the bar.

Later that night, when I told Nikki she just had a stricken look on her face. I suppose that there was no way that she wouldn't take something like that personal. But she didn't cry. She finally gave me a wry grin. "This baby is all yours." I nodded.

"No doubt."

NIKKI

Our house was still a work in progress even though it had been a month since we'd moved in. The kitchen, bathrooms and baby's room was all that we'd completed. We were at a temporary impasse on how to decorate the living room since we both had different styles. We were still going through catalogues waiting to get to something where we both went 'WOW'.

I was huge and that more than anything is what eventually caused me to put my real estate business on hold. My due date had finally come ... and then it passed. Now I went to the doctor twice a week and he told me that if I went a full week over-do then he would just take the baby. The last few days had been miserable; my feet swelled, my back ached, I looked and felt awkward and I had to pee damn near every fifteen minutes.

T rubbed my belly one night as I tried to sleep. "You know, each day that you're over-do means that I'm more likely the one that fathered the baby."

"Maybe. But the doctor says that it's typical for a first pregnancy to be over-do."

"I prefer to think of it my way if, you don't mind."

"I don't mind, baby." I yawned. "Can you rub the small of my back?"

"Achy?" He got up and kneeled in bed.

I nodded. "I can't get comfortable."

"Roll onto your side." I did and felt his fingers pressing into my sore muscles. "You're tight." He moved his fingers around my waist and to my stomach. "Stop tensing and just relax."

"I am relaxing."

He rubbed my back again. "That! You keep tensing up. Am I hurting you?"

I looked over my shoulders at him. "No my back hurts."

He climbed out of bed. "I'll make you some tea then I'll give you a full rub down."

"I love being married to a masseuse-OW!" I sucked in a sharp breath.

Tony stopped in his tracks. "Cramp?"

"No." I stared at him. "I think it was a contraction."

"Oh ... " he whispered in a voice that I could barely hear.

It wasn't until the next morning that my contractions were close enough for me to finally go to the hospital. By that time I was exhausted. Tony kept trying to get me to go to sleep but how could I? I'd been waiting for this moment for damn near half a year and there was no way that I could sleep ... and that's not even considering the pain. Only a person under the influence of severe drugs could sleep through the pain of contractions.

"I was thinking of names." Tony said, almost urgently as he drove us to the hospital. I stopped in the middle of bracing through another sharp contraction and I stared at him. He hadn't suggested any names and I hadn't pushed the issue. He'd been great in so many ways that that I didn't want to rock the boat.

"What names do you have?"

"Just two; Jade if she's a girl." I liked Jade. "And Anthony for a boy."

I looked at him. "Anthony."

"Yeah, I figured we could both be Tony. He could be T-baby, too."

"Jade and T-Baby Yakamoto." I squeezed my eyes closed and grunted though another contraction. "I like it, honey." I panted. "Ooooo … " I groaned.

He put his hand over my clenched fist. "We're almost there."

"We should have taken Lamaze class!" I yelled. At the time that Tony had suggested it, I had told him that I wasn't going to any class to learn how to breath and stretch when my body would know exactly what to do. Now I see that my body does not know what to do. It's just screaming out in pain!

I knew that labor was going to be painful, but I had no idea that it would be this particular type of pain that you can't move out of; someone stepping on your back, twisting your intestines, kicking you in your bladder, punching your uterus and shoving a lead pipe up your rectum. Why is it that no one can put into words this pain the way I just did? At least I could have been prepared for it.

But I got medicine for the pain and soon it was manageable again. It was a good thing because visitors began coming by; Mom and Dad, Mr and Mrs Y, Mrs Durdak, Shaunda and Belinda and even Jay. For a while it was busy. But it helped take my mind off things.

But soon the nurse had to usher everyone out so that she could examine me and at almost noon I was finally wheeled into delivery. When we were in the room and they were getting everything set up I began crying like an idiot. The nurses thought it was because I was afraid and started giving me words of encouragement. But Tony knew why I was crying and he just silently wiped away my tears and kissed me until I felt better. He was such a good man and I knew without a doubt that he would accept this child as his even if he hadn't fathered it ... but I wanted this baby to be his. I began praying to God. Please let this baby be his ...

"Okay Mom. I see your baby's head. I want you to push for me..."

TONY

Nikki had been pushing for half an hour, but the baby would not come out. The head was there but the baby was stuck. The doctor said that it was a really big baby. He began preparing for a C-section and Nikki protested.

"Mom, the problem is that the baby can't stay in the birth canal for very long. If it looks like it's in distress we have to do it. And right now, Mom, it looks like baby is having some distress."

Nikki reached out and gripped my hand and then things began moving fast. They put oxygen over Nikki and she at first pushed it away thinking they intended to put her under. The nurse had to tell her several times that it was just oxygen. I looked into her eyes and they were glassy. She was absolutely exhausted. I kissed her over and over and kept whispering to her that it was almost over.

They put up the big blue barrier sheet so that you couldn't see and I was sorta happy because I could take a lot but not them splitting my wife's belly open like an over ripe melon. But as I said it went fast and soon the doctor was holding a blue, limp baby in his hands.

"It's a boy, Mom and Dad!" The nurse laid the blue baby boy on my wife's belly and I watched it gasping for air as one nurse rubbed him briskly and another began sucking out fluid from his nose and mouth.

Nikki and I both stared at the baby in awe and then the nurse picked him up and carried him away.

"We're going to give the baby oxygen and get his lungs going. He's a little sluggish." And then I got scared. The baby hadn't cried yet. Didn't they have to cry? Nikki was squeezing my hand, a slow dawning fear appearing in her eyes also. Of all of the things that I had hoped and prayed for over the last few months, the last thing that I had considered was just to pray for a healthy baby. I felt my heart begin to sink. In my selfishness I hadn't asked God for just a healthy baby and now I was paying for it.

I began praying to both God and Buddha; please let him be okay. And then I heard him cry. It was loud and angry and I smiled. I bent down and kissed Nikki.

"He's going to be alright." I wiped away her last tears and then moved to the incubator where they were pulling a blue cap over my son's huge American head. The cap slowly popped off. There was so much black hair that it couldn't be contained. His color had returned and he was now transformed from blue to a tan and pink very fat baby. His fist waved angrily as he balled loudly, his perfectly formed testicles and penis all perfection. One lone tear found its way down his cheek and he opened his eyes and took a deep breath in order to draw in another breath to scream again. Those beautiful almond shaped eyes were just like mine.

T-baby was just a big kid, which is why the Ultra sound technician had guessed him as older. He weighed in at 8 lbs 7 ozs. And as soon as he passed his APGAR test, which he passed on his second try, he was wrapped in a blanket and Nikki and I were able to hold him. I didn't mention that his eyes were like mine more than hers, and when she held him she immediately counted his fingers before even remembering to check his eyes. And when she did, I saw her look at me quickly and seeing my smile.

"I love you." She mouthed.

"I love you, too." I mouthed.

I took my wife and son home the next day. We had several friends and family come by. My Mom loved the garden and had setup an outdoor buffet with several different potstickers, dumplings and cakes. Mom shared the recipes freely and I spun around and stared at her as she was talking to Jay's mother. Now I knew what was different about my mother.

I went over to her. "Mom, can you help me in the kitchen for a sec." "Sure, son." Once in the kitchen I stared at her. "Your English has really improved over the last few months."

"Eh." She agreed.

"Mom ... "

"Tony, if we're in the kitchen we may as well make more tea, eh?" I nodded.

"You just called me Tony." I said as I put the teapot on to boil.

"That's your name, isn't it?"

I sighed. "But you're the only person that calls me Toi. If you don't call me Toi then who else will?"

Her eyes got watery and she quickly turned to the cabinet to retrieve bags of various tea leaves. "Where's the Jasmine? Americans love Jasmine." I found it for her and when I did I took her hand gently and placed the tea in it.

"Thank you, Mom."

"For what?"

"For holding my Japanese for me until I was smart enough to accept it myself, and for not backing down." I put my arm around her shoulder and hugged her petite frame. "Now I see everything so clearly."

She looked up at me with a smile. "I do too."

~EPILOGUE~

"Obasaan!" Little T-Baby yelled. His grandmother was suddenly there in the doorway of the bedroom holding a toddler cup filled with some fragrant drink. "I want my Mommy," the toddler cried.

The Asian woman lifted her sleepy grandson. "Aw, Is obasaan's babyboy kimochi warui? Here drink this, you'll feel better."

T-baby shook his head and then rubbed his ear, which was slightly red and inflamed. His grandmother gently jiggled him on her hip and then blew a soft but cool breath against it. The baby giggled, his previous tears forgotten and then reached for the cup of juice and drank it down.

"Oishii." he gasped breathlessly after having drank every drop.

"Yes it is good!" She said proudly. He received a kiss on his cheek from his grandmother who then carried him into the dining room where a gathering of women were seated at the table containing Mahjong tiles, a plate of almond cookies and half filled cups of tea.

Everyone oohed and ahhed at the little brown two year old with his head of big black curls and eyes as almond shaped as their own.

"Oh let me hold him, Kayo."

"No, me. I haven't held him yet."

"No, it's time for his medicine," she responded. Someone complained that she got to keep him five days a week while his parents worked. But Mrs Yakamoto didn't care. They could hold their own grandbabies and she would hold hers! Kayo Yakamoto reached into the refrigerator for T-baby's Amoxicillin.

Once the ladies determined that she would be stingy with her grandchild the conversation switched to other things.

"Mrs Lee bought a piano for her ungrateful son and daughter-in-law."

"A piano?"

"Yes, and none of them play!"

The women chattered away as Mrs Yakamoto used the baby syringe to squirt some of the medicine into the baby's unsuspecting mouth.

He screwed up his little brown face to the laughter of the other women and was immediately rewarded with a cookie.

Mrs Tonisho waved her hand and scowled. "Western medicine only works on Westerners. Take a warm mug and place it against his ear with a hot wash towel-"

"No, mineral oil works best!"

"He has a cold not swimmers ear." Mrs Yakamoto scowled but good-naturedly. "Ginger, lemon and honey mixed in with his juice."

"Ah, he will have the poops for sure."

She sat down with her grandson, arranging her tiles while T-Baby drooled over his cookie. Mrs Yakamoto jiggled him on her knee and then smiled to herself.

THE END

Miscegenist Sabishii

PEPPER PACE BOOKS

STRANDED!
Juicy
Love Intertwined Vol. 1
Love Intertwined Vol. 2
Urban Vampire; The Turning
Urban Vampire; Creature of the Night
Urban Vampire; The Return of Alexis
Wheels of Steel Book 1
Wheels of Steel Book 2
Wheels of Steel Book 3
Wheels of Steel Book 4
Angel Over My Shoulder
CRASH
Miscegenist Sabishii
They Say Love Is Blind
Beast
A Seal Upon Your Heart
Everything is Everything Book 1
Everything is Everything Book 2
Adaptation
About Coco's Room

SHORT STORIES

~~***~~

Someone to Love
The Way Home
MILF
Blair and the Emoboy
Emoboy the Submissive Dom
1-900-BrownSugar
Someone To Love
My Special Friend
Baby Girl and the Mean Boss
A Wrong Turn Towards Love
The Delicate Sadness
The Shadow People
The Love Unexpected

COLLABORATIONS

~~***~~

Seduction: An Interracial Romance
Anthology Vol. 1
Scandalous Heroes Box set

About the Author

Pepper Pace creates a unique brand of Interracial/multicultural erotic romance. While her stories span the gamut from humorous to heartfelt, the common theme is crossing racial boundaries.

The author is comfortable in dealing with situations that are, at times, considered taboo. Readers find themselves questioning their own sense of right and wrong, attraction and desire. The author believes that an erotic romance should first begin with romance and only then does she offers a look behind the closed doors to the passion.

Pepper Pace lives in Cincinnati, Ohio where many of her stories take place. She writes in the genres of science fiction, youth, horror, urban lit and poetry. She is a member of several online role-playing groups and hosts several blogs. In addition to writing, the author is also an artist, an introverted recluse, a self proclaimed empath and a foodie. Pepper Pace can be contacted at her blog, Writing Feedback: http://pepperpacefeedback.blogspot.com/ PepperPace.tumblr.com **or by email at** pepperpace.author@yahoo.com

Miscegenist Sabishii

Awards

Pepper Pace is a best selling author on Amazon and AllRomance e-books as well as Literotica.com. She is the winner of the 11th Annual Literotica Awards for 2009 for Best Reluctance story, as well as best Novels/Novella. She is also recipient of Literotica's August 2009 People's Choice Award, and was awarded second place in the January 2010 People's Choice Award. In the 12th Annual Literotica Awards for 2010, Pepper Pace won number one writer in the category of Novels/Novella as well as best interracial story. Pepper has also made notable accomplishments at Amazon. In 2013 she twice made the list of top 100 Erotic Authors and has reached the top 10 best sellers in multiple genres as well as placing in the semi-finals in the 2013 Amazon Breakthrough Author's contest.

Made in the USA
Middletown, DE
05 July 2021